# GO
# FIGURE

# Also by Jo Edwards

*Love Undercover*

# GO FIGURE

## jo edwards

**SIMON PULSE**

NEW YORK    LONDON    TORONTO    SYDNEY

This book is a work of fiction. Any references to historical events, real
people, or real locales are used fictitiously. Other names, characters,
places, and incidents are the product of the author's imagination, and
any resemblance to actual events or locales or persons, living or dead,
is entirely coincidental.

SIMON PULSE

An imprint of Simon & Schuster Children's Publishing Division

1230 Avenue of the Americas, New York, NY 10020

Copyright © 2007 by Johanna Edwards

All rights reserved, including the right of reproduction

in whole or in part in any form.

SIMON PULSE and colophon are registered trademarks of

Simon & Schuster, Inc.

The text of this book was set in Sabon.

Manufactured in the United States of America

First Simon Pulse edition October 2007

2  4  6  8  10  9  7  5  3  1

Library of Congress Control Number 2007924079

ISBN-13: 978-1-4169-2492-0

ISBN-10: 1-4169-2492-2

*For my sister, Selena,*
*who is my constant friend,*
*as well as partner in crime*

# GO
# FIGURE

# Acknowledgments

THANK YOU, THANK YOU, THANK YOU TO JENNY Bent. In addition to being a top-notch agent, Jenny's a terrific friend. I owe much (if not all) of my success to her. My editor, Michelle Nagler, never ceases to amaze me with her brilliance. Thanks also to Jenny's assistant, Victoria Horn, and to Michelle's assistant, Michael del Rosario. And a huge thank-you to Caroline Abbey. Much love to everyone at Simon Pulse for working so hard on the book!

Thanks to my mother, Paula Edwards, and my father, Les Edwards. Thanks to Rachel Worthington for being such an awesome pal and for putting up with my crazy middle-of-the-night phone calls. Thanks to James Abbott for reminding me to always "check it with Bully" so I don't make any spelling mistakes. Thanks to Jeff Williams for giving me the sperm . . . bank info. Thanks to Chris "Tom and Jordan" Carwile, who has been there from day one of my writing career. And I owe so much to my mentor, Candy Justice, whose advice, guidance, and humor mean the world to me.

Thanks also go out to: Selena Edwards, Hugo Reynolds, Teresa Johnson, Anastasia Nix, Velda Nix, Paul Turner, Alan Turner, Sallie Turner, Eva Edwards, Leslie Edwards, Helen Turner, Leo Edwards, Bert Edwards, Tommy Edwards, Laura Turner, Waymon Turner, Valerie Gildart, Emily Trenholm, Erin Hiller, Virginia Feltus, Susanne Enos, Dr. James Patterson, Jay Eubanks, Christy Paganoni, Dr. Cynthia Hopson, Kate Simone, Matt Presson, Stephen Usery, Cheryl Hudson, Paul "Diners Club" Simone, Runi Afsharpour Perkins, Christie Bangloy, Alan Klein, Debra Hall, Alicia Funkhouser, Melissa Stroud, Demonica Santangilo, Nikki Hatchel, Maralou Billig, Lynn Kloker, Debby Mirda, Donna Pineau, Paula Rogers, and Tiffany Werne. And in loving memory of my friend William Clanton.

# Prologue

I WAS TEN YEARS OLD WHEN I STOPPED BEING SKINNY.

It didn't happen overnight, but it sure felt that way. As if one moment I was thin and happy and perfect, and the next I was getting picked last for kickball, shopping in the plus-size department, and hopping on the scale at Weight Watchers (they have a special program for teens).

I guess the weight crept on slowly, pound after pound, just like it always does. And I guess I had some choice in the matter—I could have eaten carrot sticks instead of fries, a turkey sandwich in lieu of pizza. (But, really, is life without chocolate and pizza worth living? I think not!)

But the whole thing felt so sudden and, I must say, beyond my control.

It was at cheerleading camp that I was first outted as a fat girl.

Yes, cheerleading camp.

This should tell you that I didn't know my own girth. No self-respecting chubette would ever sign up for three months of herkies, somersaults, and human pyramids. Not to mention butt-cheek-length skirts and weekly weigh-ins. Ah, the weigh-ins. They were the bane of my existence, even before my thighs were packed with cellulite and my butt jiggled when I walked.

But it was not the scale that betrayed me.

It was Sadie (who, for all intents and purposes, might as well have been named Sadist). She was the first person ever to call me fat.

Sadie was a bubbly twenty-three-year-old who went to the University of Tennessee at Knoxville on a cheerleading scholarship. After failing to land a cheering job with any of the pro teams, Sadie moved to Atlanta and began teaching preteen gymnastics and cheering.

My mother signed me up for Sadie's day camp the summer before my sixth-grade year. Things were pretty bad in our family back then, and my mom was looking for a way to cheer me up (pun intended).

My brother, Mark, had been diagnosed with leukemia a few months earlier, and my whole family had more or less stopped functioning. I spent a lot of time by myself that year, eating Cheetos for dinner, watching TV to help me fall asleep, while my mom huddled next to Mark's bed at the hospital.

It was during that period that I got fat. I'm not blaming my brother's illness; I know it's not his fault. But if I had to draw out a timeline of when my body took a turn for the worse, Mark's cancer would be the point where it started.

The point where it blew up in my face was a Monday afternoon in July. We were practicing round-off back-handsprings when I took a big spill. I stood up, dusted myself off, and hobbled over to Sadie so she could examine my bum ankle.

But she was much more interested in my body as a whole.

"No wonder you fell. At this rate, you're not going to be able to do that move for much longer," Sadie said, pointing a finger at my stomach. "Your last weigh-in showed you at a hundred and twenty-eight pounds," she announced. Out loud. For everyone to hear.

There were audible gasps. We were fifth graders. There were girls on the squad who weighed less than seventy pounds.

"You're gettin' *really* fat, girlie. Really fat," Sadie said again, just in case anyone had missed it the first time. She squeezed my upper arm with her manicured fingers. "And it's affecting your tumbling in a *big* way. You'd better start

3

watching what you eat, pronto. You don't want to grow up and look like Carnie Wilson."

I didn't even know who Carnie Wilson was, but when I looked her up on the Internet that night, I was horrified. This was a woman so gargantuan, the doctors had to seal off most of her stomach; so fat, she needed weight-loss surgery just to live.

Was this really where I was headed? Was I really that big? I was suddenly acutely aware of my body in a way I never had been before. I was aware that I didn't measure up.

Instead of getting motivated, I threw in the towel. I stopped caring. No one in my family was around. No one was watching. It just didn't seem to matter. And it was easier to enjoy a piece of chocolate cake *right this minute* than to eat apples and broccoli every day and night so that a year or two in the future my body would be slimmer. It felt like a lost cause.

Things started going downhill rapidly.

Now that Sadie had called me fat, the other girls started doing it too, and none of the coaches stopped them.

"Fat ass!"

"Whale!"

"Bubble butt!"

They'd squeal and make *oink-oink* noises when I ran down the mat in tumbling practice.

"Look at that piggy go!"

"Jiggle all the way!"

"I'm surprised she doesn't bust through the floorboards."

I quit soon after that.

Seven years—and more than seventy pounds—later, here I am.

Fat.

Really, and truly, fat.

I turned to photography after I left cheerleading behind. It was a natural fit for me. I like capturing life. And as long as I'm the one taking the pictures, I don't have to be in them. I don't like being in them.

My shrink would tell you I have intimacy issues.

I see Dr. Paige on Mondays. For a long time I thought this was her last name, but it's actually not. Her last name is Norris, but she insists on being called Dr. Paige. I guess she's trying to be sleek and hip, like Dr. Phil or something.

Dr. Paige is a psychologist *and* a psychiatrist. This is quite a unique achievement. She has a PhD and an MD. Which means she can both talk me into a stupor and ply me with pills.

It was my pediatrician, Dr. Gibbons, who first noticed I seemed stressed and anxious.

"Ryan's showing signs of depression," he told my mom, while I sat there, squirming around in his office chair. I hate when people discuss me like I'm not there. I also hate Dr. Gibbons's chairs, which are about as roomy and comfortable as your standard airplane seat. (I guess that's what I get for going to a pediatrician at sixteen.) "She's not sleeping, she's having trouble concentrating on her work, and she feels hopeless sometimes, like her life will never come together," he said. "Oh, and her eating's very disordered."

Great. There it was again. It seemed I couldn't go five minutes without my weight cropping up in the conversation.

"I think Ryan could really benefit from medication, cognitive therapy, or both." He suggested Zoloft, and my mother balked.

"Ryan's only sixteen! How can she need Zoloft *at sixteen*?"

"Depression is not an age-specific condition," Dr. Gibbons said. "It affects the young and the old. And it's quite common in adolescent girls." He recited some disturbing statistics about teenagers and mental health. Ten minutes later my mother was on the phone, booking an appointment for me with Dr. Paige.

"She's very good," Dr. Gibbons said, writing out a prescription for 50 mgs of Zoloft. As an afterthought, he gave me Klonopin, which is a smooth little antianxiety med. It's nice stuff. I could probably make a pretty penny selling it at school if I wanted to. But I don't. I'd rather take them. "I think you'll find Dr. Paige's treatment beneficial."

I didn't.

"Give it some time," Mom said.

It's been six months, and I still find the sessions grating.

Dr. Paige is young and perky and full of opinions. She didn't like the fact that Dr. Gibbons gave me Zoloft and Klonopin, though she agreed to keep me on them for the time being. She's a big fan of talk therapy, and her method of treatment involves role-playing games ("I'll be your mother, and you practice saying all the things you've been holding back") and homework assignments. She has a tear-off notepad that says FREUDIAN SLIPS on the top and has her name stamped underneath that. Each week she writes down a goal for me to complete over the next seven days.

Sometimes they're silly: *Eat an ice-cream sundae in public!* Sometimes they're tedious: *Draw an emotional timeline, showing how your weight has changed in relation to your feelings*. But they usually involve food, my body, or some combination of the two.

I know how pathetic this probably sounds, but, rest assured, this is not a sad story. Oh, there are dark parts in it, to be sure.

But it's like my mother likes to say: It's always darkest before the dawn. I've never been a fan of that phrase. It's cheesy, clichéd. And I'm not much of an optimist, even on my best days. I'm cynical. Easily depressed. And I always think I have the world figured out. (A lot of the time it seems like I do.)

But every once in a while the world throws me a curveball, the kind of hit you never see coming.

I guess this was one of those things; *he* was one of those things.

Because I never could have seen him—never could have seen any of this—coming.

# Freudian Slips

## DR. PAIGE NORRIS, PhD, MD

PATIENT: *Ryan Burke*

PERSONAL GOALS FOR THE WEEK

1. You have a bad habit of blaming everything on your weight. So for the next seven days, you must embrace your fat, forgive it.

2. Do not eat in secret. All meals must be consumed in front of other people.

# Chapter One

MY EX-BOYFRIEND IS ON THE COVER OF THIS week's *Rolling Stone*.

He's wearing a pair of Dolce & Gabbana shredded jeans, a $300 Christian Audigier T-shirt, and the dollar-store bracelet I gave him for his seventeenth birthday.

I know how this looks. I swear I'm not a cheapskate. And, no, I wasn't trying to turn him gay.

Noah asked me for that bracelet. Demanded it, really. We were goofing around at Just-a-Buck in downtown Atlanta one day after school when he spied it: a shiny, faux-silver charm bracelet with the Pisces emblem dangling from the end. You know the one: two fish swimming in opposite directions—one against the current, one with it.

It was gaudy, oversize costume jewelry—the kind of thing a little kid might wear. Or a drag queen.

But Noah loved it anyway. "You know, my birthday's next

week," he'd hinted, nudging me in the side. "You keep asking for suggestions of what to get me. . . . Well, get this."

So I bought the bracelet. Against my better judgment, I might add. When he wore it to school a few weeks later, a couple of the jock guys wasted no time pouncing on him.

"That's like advertising you're a pussy," one of them said, leaning over and tugging on the fish. "A full-fledged girlie girl."

I cringed, but Noah laughed it off. He was such a geek back then, but he didn't care. (Nowadays, I bet there's a million guys lining up to get those zodiac bracelets, just because they saw Noah wear it on the cover of *RS*.) It was one of the things that made Noah so unique—his ability to not care what anyone thought. Although, at times, he went a tad too far. Like when, after being elected president of the French club, he started wearing a beret. To school. Every single day. Kind of embarrassing, to be sure, but that was just Noah. He did his own thing: watched dorky cartoons, listened to geeky music, played in the jazz band.

Of course, you see where it's gotten him now. A record deal with BMG. A Grammy nomination for Best New Artist (he didn't win). The aforementioned *Rolling Stone* cover, complete with the headline "Can Noah Fairbanks Save Pop Music?" Which is kind of stupid, since most people classify him as more folk than pop, but whatever. His debut album, *Conundrum*, went platinum, and he's supposedly raking in eight figures a year.

And to think, I've seen this guy naked.

But before we go further, here's what you need to know about our relationship.

**Name:** Noah Michael Fairbanks

**Dated:** Fourteen months. For all of my freshmen (his junior) year and part of tenth grade.

**The vital stats:** Ordinarily, dating an upperclassman brings you some form of notoriety. This did not happen when I started seeing Noah. As I've already said, he was not a cool guy back then, and going out with him didn't do much to help my social status.

He broke up with me during his senior year because he felt "our relationship had run its course" and it was time to move on. What he really meant was that he wanted to move on to Meredith, a cute redhead who likely weighed 102 pounds soaking wet.

And, no, despite what pretty much every person who knows me thinks, I am not obsessed with Noah.

I'm not.

Admittedly, there's a part of me that's living vicariously through him. I can't help but wonder what would have happened if we'd never broken up. Would he take me to the Grammys? Write songs for me? Bring me along on his world tour? Pay for my liposuction? (Okay, so I'm not serious about that last one—but every plus-size gal dreams about getting a little lipo on her butt now and then.)

But, I'll say it again. I am not obsessing!

**I love yous:** He said it on our six-month anniversary. I returned it. Don't know for sure if either of us really meant it.

**Sex:** No, I didn't sleep with him. We went to what I guess is called third base. (I'm really bad when it comes to this kind of stuff. I know first is kissing and second is boobing. But what's third? Because if it's what I think it is . . . hands wandering everywhere . . . then they really need to switch metaphors. There's some kind of important stuff that happens after third, and before fourth, yet we have no way to describe it.)

**Degree that my <u>fat</u> hindered the relationship, on a scale of 1 to 10: 5.**

That last category probably seems weird, but you've got to understand. I measure everything—every relationship, every goal—by how much my fat interferes. Because, believe me, the sneaky bugger's always getting in the way.

(Dr. Paige would have a fit if she saw this topic. Dr. Paige thinks I am letting my fat rule my life and that I have to stop blaming all of my problems on it. The woman is truly nuts. My goal for this week is to "embrace my fat." I find it gross enough to let someone else embrace it; why would I want to do it myself?)

Now, it's not that I'm naive enough to believe being thin would make me perfect, or that I'd magically get everything I wanted if I lost sixty pounds.

And I also don't believe my friends and family are that shallow. I don't think they dislike me because I'm overweight. But I can't help but wonder—would they like me BETTER if I were thin? Would they respect me more, see me as a viable contender? Sometimes it feels like I'm coming at life with a disadvantage. If I were thin, the playing field would be level. Right now I don't think it is. . . .

Noah never bugged me to lose weight. That's one thing I really loved about him. My other boyfriends haven't all been so accepting.

I'll give you the deets about *them* a little later on. But right now, let's get back to the *Rolling Stone* article.

I'm quoted in it, you know. Page 57.

*"Noah's a hearts and flowers kind of guy, a real romantic,"* says former girlfriend Ryan Burke. *"He remembers every anniversary, every birthday. He makes you hot chocolate when it's cold out, writes love poems, buys you little gifts just because."*

I made Noah sound great, right? Or so I thought.

But the journalist poked fun at my statements, following up with: *Burke stops short of calling Fairbanks an all-out God, although she makes sure to let it slip that, in his spare time, the singer likes to volunteer at soup kitchens and animal shelters. It's hard to tell if Burke is genuine, or if she's just feeding into the carefully crafted PR machine that is Noah Fairbanks.*

Kind of harsh, isn't it? At least they spelled my name right. And they didn't misidentify me as a guy, which happens now and again.

Why my mother named me Ryan, I'll never know. I didn't even get a girl's middle name. I'm Ryan Braeden Burke. What the hell?

I questioned my mom about it once, and her answer was beyond dumb. "I love boys names," she said simply. "Would you rather be named something predictable like Mary or Cathy or Anne?"

*Yes, Mom. Yes, I would.*

"Ryan has character, personality. Besides, I picked out the name long before you were born. Long before I knew if you'd be an XX or an XY."

This would make more sense if I'd been an only child, or the last in a long line of girls, you know, and she'd called me Ryan because it was her all-time favorite guy name and she never got to use it. But I have an older brother, Mark, which throws that theory out the window.

This is why you need two parents.

Yes, you heard me right. I only have one parent. My father was a sperm donor. I'm not being cagey. My dad is not some bastard who walked out while I was still in diapers and I've taken to calling him a sperm donor because I can't stand to speak his name.

I don't even know his name.

My mother, a thoroughly modern woman of the world, decided that she didn't need a man for anything. Procreation included. So she went to the sperm bank in the mid eighties and—voila!—nine months later, she had Mark. A few years after that, she headed back for seconds and along I came.

Mom is damn proud of the fact that she's a strong, liberated, non-penis-needing woman. She tells everyone, I mean, absolutely everyone—from our postman to my third-grade teacher—that she was a sperm bank recipient.

Personally, I find the whole thing creepy. Rather than being the product of love, or marriage, or even booze-filled lust, I am the product of specimen cups and test tubes and dirty magazines. Yikes. Some guy jacked off to *Playboy* so that I could be conceived. It's disgusting, if you think about it.

Speaking of disgusting, I once read an article about "The World's Most Prolific Sperm Donor." Apparently, some guy in the Midwest makes a donation, on average, once a week. He's been doing this for several decades. They even named a wing after him at the sperm bank. According to the story, he probably has several thousand kids roaming around the United States by now. He has a few natural children with his wife, and there's a legitimate concern that some of his offspring may one day bump into one another. I remember one of his quotes in the article freaked me out:

"My kids will have to be really careful when they start dating. They should probably take a DNA kit along with them. There's the distinct possibility that they could wind up getting involved with one of their half siblings and not even know it."

Knowing my luck, I got that guy's swimmers. And I'll meet some hot, Brad Pitt–looking guy (why is it always Brad Pitt?)

only to discover on our wedding night that we're actually sperm bank siblings.

See, these are the kinds of things my mother should have thought about before she ran off and got inseminated.

Dr. Paige says I have Daddy issues, and maybe that's true.

I hate that I'll never know my father. I'll never know if he gave me my blue eyes or my big nose or my short stature. I'm pretty sure I got my fat gene from him. Both Mom and Mark are stick figures. I actually worked it out once. Based on my family's appearance (the half I know), my birth father must have been a real ogre. Everyone on my mom's side of the family is tall and thin and exotic looking. High cheekbones and blond hair and petite little noses. My real dad must have been about five foot two, with brown hair, a giant honker, and a huge gut. I kind of picture him looking like Danny DeVito. Danny DeVito as the Penguin in *Batman Returns*, which, incidentally, came out around the same time I was born.

There are a million other bad things about being a sperm donor baby, but I won't get into all of that right now.

Right now I'm waiting on a ride. I'm standing outside the mall clutching a Torrid bag. It's about 700 degrees outside— typical Atlanta August—and beads of sweat are rolling down my back.

I wish she'd hurry up and get here. She being Kimberlee Johnston, my pseudo best friend. Kimberlee and I got to know each other this past summer while we were both working at DigiHut, a camera shop located in an outlet mall near my house. She's a pretty cool girl, but I never could have predicted we'd become such good friends.

For starters, we don't have a lot in common. I go to Greenlee High, a public school that has nearly two thousand students. Kimberlee goes to a tiny Catholic school, which she hates. "The dress code sucks ass," she often complains. There's the requisite Catholic schoolgirl uniform, of course, but that's not what bugs Kim most. She's not allowed to wear any wild jewelry or do anything funky with her hair. When I first met her at the beginning of the summer, her hair was dyed a shade of red that bordered on purple. She's had to dye it back to its natural brown, since school's starting again in a few days.

Kim's outgoing—she's on her school's dance squad and her cell phone never stops ringing. She's also got a perfect figure, which I find impossible to relate to.

Kimberlee and I are close by default—we both recently lost our constant companions. Her boyfriend, Taylor, just started college in Vermont. They're doing the long-distance thing. Ever since he left, Kim's been feeling really lonely. Those two were joined at the hip for most of high school, and she doesn't know what to do now that he's gone. I didn't lose a boyfriend, but I did lose Chelsea, my BFFF (best fat friend forever). Chelsea and I have been inseparable since the eighth grade. She left in June to spend the summer with her father out in California. The trip was last minute, unexpected. I've missed her like crazy. Thank God she'll be back in time to start senior year.

A car horn honks, shaking me from my reverie.

"What's up, *chica*?"

It's Kimberlee. She's got this bizarre habit of calling every girl *chica* and every guy *hombre*. It makes no sense, considering her lineage is Russian.

I grab my bag and run over to her car—a silver Mercedes C320. It's a hand-me-down from her parents. Instead of trading in their five-year-old car, they let Kim have it. My mom thinks it's ridiculous that a seventeen-year-old was handed a luxury car like that. I think it rocks. I open the passenger's side door and climb in, my legs sticking to the leather seats.

"Thanks for picking me up."

"No problem." She grabs the gearshift with gusto and throws it into first. The car nearly stalls out, then lurches forward.

"You've had this thing for, what, three months?" I ask.

"Five."

"And you still haven't gotten the hang of driving a stick?"

"I'm doing juuuuuust fine." She laughs. "I haven't hit anybody yet. And I haven't rolled backward into any parked cars."

A minute later we're bouncing down the road, the radio blaring.

"I'm dying for some caffeine, you wanna go to the coffee shop?" she shouts over the music.

"Yeah, sounds great!"

"What'd you buy at the mall?"

I self-consciously tuck the Torrid bag under my feet. "Just a shirt and a few pairs of jeans." Size twenty, but I don't tell her this.

"Good idea, getting a new outfit for the party," she says, grinning at me. "I still haven't figured out what I'm going to wear to Max's."

Max Steadman is pretty much the coolest guy who ever lived. Well, the coolest guy who ever lived on my block, anyway. Every year he throws this massive back-to-school party that usually starts on Friday night and ends sometime around six a.m. Sunday morning—just in time for Max to get the place cleaned up before his mom returns from spending the weekend at her boyfriend's house in Birmingham. For the past three years, Max's mother has been having a long-distance relationship with a (married!) guy she met online. They spend nearly every weekend holed up in a hotel in Alabama, leaving Max home alone with his mom's stash of booze and weed. "Fucking Match dot com made me the most popular guy in school!" Max often jokes.

It's one of the biggest social events of the year.

But I didn't buy the new clothes for Max's party. "I actually got these for the first day of school," I tell Kimberlee.

"Ugh, don't remind me. I can't believe summer's almost over." Kim groans. "At least you guys get to start next Wednesday. Private schools start this Monday."

"I know. That sucks."

"Anyway, let me see what you bought." She reaches over, grasping for the bag.

"Not while you're driving!" I shriek. "Once we stop." *And once I have the chance to cut the tags out,* I add silently.

Kimberlee grows bored with the song on the radio—something by Jack's Mannequin—and pops in an Evanescence CD. She sings along, trying miserably to match Amy Lee's range. Two shrill songs later and we're there.

23

We walk into the coffee shop, grab two drinks to go, and then get back into the car.

"So," she asks, slurping on an iced caramel latte, "Noah's new single is out soon. And his CD comes out in October. What are we doing to celebrate?"

"Celebrate?" I ask, taking a tentative sip of my iced coffee.

"Yeah! I know you're going to the big CD release party in New York."

I am? "Not exactly . . ."

"But what are we doing here?" she continues, ignoring me. "When is Noah coming into town? Are you throwing him some kind of bash?"

"Whoa, whoa, whoa." I hold up a hand to stop her. "I've told you this a billion times. I talk to Noah, like, three times a year. I have no idea when—and if—he's coming back to Atlanta. And I seriously doubt I'll get an invite to his launch party."

"Come on." She shakes the ice around in her drink. "I know you keep insisting you guys aren't tight." She gives me a look that says, *I don't believe you.* "But you're always quoted in the articles about him. And you always seem to know what he's up to way before anybody else does. I understand you don't want people taking advantage of your . . . connection . . . to a celebrity. But I'm not that way. I'm not gonna, like, use you to get close to Noah Fairbanks."

This is true. In fact, when we first met, Kimberlee had no idea about my connection to Noah. I kept it that way on purpose; it was nice having a friend who wanted to know about *me* instead of my ex-boyfriend. She found out about me and Noah a few weeks ago, when my brother mentioned it. (It's been pleasantly surprising, though. Kim doesn't fawn over Noah the way most people do.)

"I know you're not, but I'm telling you the truth. I have a current e-mail address for Noah and a cell phone number that's a few months out of date. Who knows if it's still even accurate? He changes it, like, every couple of weeks."

"When was the last time you talked?"

"A few weeks ago," I admit. "He e-mailed me to see how it went when the journalist from *Rolling Stone* called me."

"That's so awesome how the press always calls you."

"The reason they call me is because I was Noah's first girlfriend."

"Noah's *only* girlfriend," she chimes in.

My face blushes red.

"You were each other's firsts, weren't you?" She turns to

25

face me and cocks an eyebrow. "Was he good? Was he . . . you know, sportin' a big one?"

"Okay—enough, enough!" I giggle nervously. "Not going there." Not that there was anywhere *to* go. Noah and I were both virgins when we started dating—and we remained that way when we broke up.

We get back to Kimberlee's house and head inside. We say a quick hello to her younger brother, then trudge upstairs to watch TV. Kim snacks on candy while I chew a piece of sugar-free gum. She has a giant bowl of mini chocolate bars on her nightstand—a fact that amazes me. How does someone eat these things and not gain an ounce? Where does it go?

"Here," Kimberlee throws me the remote control. "I'm going to grab a shower." She strips down, dropping trou right in front of me.

"Kim!"

"What?"

"You're . . . !" I avert my eyes. Things like this always make me uncomfortable. I guess I'm so shy about my own body that it freaks me out to see other people being so flower child about nudity.

Plus, I've heard rumors before that Kim swings both ways.

Who knows if it's true? It was Andy, the assistant manager at DigiHut, who told me. And, given how horny he was, I don't trust much of what he said. His tales of Kimberlee's wild sexual exploits may have been pure fantasy.

Still, I'm not down with this nudity thing.

"Can you put some clothes on?"

Kimberlee looks at herself in the mirror. "Sorry. I'm used to dance squad, remember? We all walk around buck-ass naked in the locker room. Nobody cares."

I sneak a peak and it depresses me. She's so thin and tanned and toned. Even if I lose all the weight I need to— around seventy pounds—I bet my body will still be lumpy and weird and disproportionate. Nothing like hers. Kim could model for Victoria's Secret, her body's that good.

She ducks into the bathroom, and I hear the water start up. "So I'm thinking about putting an ad on one of those online dating things."

"What?" I say, confused. "What about Taylor?"

"What about him?" She steps back into her bedroom. This time, mercifully, there's a towel wrapped around her chest.

"I thought you guys were doing the long-distance thing?"

"Oh, we totally are." She runs a brush through her long brown hair, then clips it up on top of her head. "But that doesn't mean I don't have needs. I need to get the job done, you know. And I'm not into the whole self-service thing. . . ."

I sigh. "Kim, there are at least fifty guys at my school who'd be glad 'get the job done' for you."

She smiles. "Maybe. But then it'd get back to Taylor. He went to Greenlee, remember? The last thing I need are a bunch of rumors swirling around. I want to get in and out." She laughs. "Well, I guess that's his job."

"But online dating?" I groan, thinking of Max Steadman's mom and her married man. "Why don't you just buy a vibrator?"

"I have one," she says, and I can't tell if she's joking or not.

"Can't you meet a guy somewhere else, then?"

"Not the kind of guy I want."

"Which is?"

"A college guy."

"You already have one of those."

"Yeah, one who lives eight thousand miles away."

"More like eight hundred."

"I want an Athens boy."

"UGA?"

She nods. "University of Georgia boys are so f'ing hot.

And they're close, but not too close. I can drive down there on the weekends, get my stuff done, and then ditch him as soon as it's over." She rubs her hands together and smiles wickedly. "It's the perfect plan!"

"Sounds like it." I pick a piece of lint off my T-shit.

"Are you in?"

"Excuse me?"

"Will you get on the site with me? Look for a guy for yourself?"

I jolt to attention. "No way."

"Ryan. Pleaaaaase?"

"No. Honestly. I can't do that. It's too creepy." Plus, the whole online world scares me. Too much potential for lying. I don't trust anyone out there—myself included. "Match dot com and all those sites are really sleazy. And I doubt they let you on unless you're eighteen, maybe twenty-one. So you'll have to lie about your age."

"I was going to do that, anyway," she says, fixing me with an annoyed stare. "Most college boys are terrified of jailbait, so I'm gonna bump it up a year or two." Kim thinks it over. "But you're probably right. Having an ad online screams desperate wench. I think I'll Facebook it. I'm sure I can find a guy that way."

"Definitely."

Kim wags a finger at me. "But I'm not going to let you off the hook this easy. While I'm on there looking for myself I'll be keeping my eyes peeled for you."

"I'm not going to have a one-night stand," I blurt out.

"Chill, *chica*. Who said anything about one-night stands?"

"You did," I remind her.

"Well, that was for me. You're a different issue. You, like, never have sex."

She's right. I don't. I definitely have some sort of weird issue when it comes to sex. For one thing, I'm not all that interested in it. Oh, sure, I have my desires just like the next girl . . . but the idea of stripping down in front of a guy freaks me out. Big-time. I don't even like being naked in private; I'd take a shower with my clothes on, if I could.

Now I know it's not PC, but I've got to blame my mom on this one. At least a little. After all, the woman has such an aversion to sex that she didn't even do it to get pregnant.

"You probably don't even masturbate."

"Okay, let's not go there."

"You know, if I had memories of being with a hot guy like Noah Fairbanks, I'd probably fantasize about him all the time too."

"Enough." I groan. "Please. Stop talking about Noah."

"All right, all right." She raises her eyebrows up and down playfully. "What you need is a make-out buddy. You guys can hold hands and snuggle and—gasp!—maybe even kiss for a little bit. Not French, though. We wouldn't want things to get too out of hand."

I stick my tongue out at her, as if to prove a point.

"Wow! It still works." Kimberlee nods approvingly. "Come on, let me find you a guy. You won't regret it, I swear."

The issue decided, she heads off to get in the shower, before I can object.

I flip through an issue of *Cosmo*, checking out a feature on the hottest diets for fall. Good God. The weight-loss industry really is a year-round machine. Now it's not good enough to shape up just for bikini season—you've gotta lose the pudge in time for bulky sweaters and baggy pants.

I skim the article and it makes me depressed. This was supposed to be *the year*. I was going to start my senior year as a thin girl. I was going to wow them. But month after month passed, and despite my goals, despite how badly I wanted it, I'm still here, doing the same old thing I've always done.

Being the same old fat girl I've always been. So many

milestones have passed—milestones I was supposed to lose weight for. They've come and gone and I haven't shed an inch. I didn't get thin in time for high school, for my first date, my sweet sixteen, my prom.

But all is not lost. If I work really hard now, I might be able to get skinny in time for graduation. I have to. Otherwise, no one from high school will ever know me as a thin person. We'll go our separate ways next year and this will be the memory they'll have. They will know me as the fat girl—and there are five at our school. They will remember me as the chick Noah Fairbanks dated before he got hot and famous and rich.

I always hope for reinvention, for redemption. But then something gets in the way. Usually something deep fried or chocolate. A moment on the lips . . . and my goal evaporates into thin air.

I hear the water stop, and I know in a minute Kimberlee will be out, probably naked. Definitely hot. She's perfect in about a thousand different ways.

Kimberlee's younger sister, Lisa, comes upstairs. She's got a friend in tow. Some blond Barbie look-alike who is all of twelve. So I guess that makes her Stacie, or whatever Barbie's little sister is called these days.

"Kim, we're going to look through your clothes, okay?" Lisa yells.

"Sure! But only the old stuff," Kim calls back. "I saw you eyeing my True Religion jeans last night, so don't you dare put your hands on those!"

"Okay, but I totally caught you wearing my red top last weekend. Don't think I didn't notice! I said you could take the *tee*, not the red cami."

This is depressing. Kim is nearly eighteen and she wears the same-size clothes as a sixth grader. I wish I were thin so I could wear Kimberlee's clothes. This has been a secret dream of mine all summer. Ever since we became friends, I've been wishing I could magically transform into a size two so I could borrow her stuff. She's incredibly generous—always offering to let me wear her C Label shoes or carry her Kate Spade bag. I know if I were skinny enough, she'd be lending me her clothes, too.

Lisa and Barbie's Younger Sister begin sorting through a pile of hand-me-downs that are laid out on the chair, separating the things they want and discarding the rest.

"Is this all right for Nikka's sleepover?" Lisa asks, and her friend nods.

"Perfect!"

They're so beautiful, both of them, and I can't help

thinking that they'll grow up like Kimberlee and lead these crazy-charmed lives.

That's what happens to beautiful people.

Oh, they can protest, they can pretend, but everyone knows the truth. Their lives are as perfect as their looks.

I reach over to the nightstand, grab a mini Snickers bar, and rip the wrapper off with my teeth.

When no one's looking, I take a bite.

# Freudian Slips

## DR. PAIGE NORRIS, PhD, MD

PATIENT: *Ryan Burke*

PERSONAL GOALS FOR THE WEEK

1. *Compile a list of misconceptions you feel people have about you because of your weight.*

# Chapter Two

AFTER HOLDING OUT FOR MORE THAN TWO months, I finally cave in and weigh myself this morning. And on a Monday, no less. Monday is the worst possible day to weigh yourself. I am inevitably carrying around *at least* three extra pounds, thanks to all the partying/pigging out I did Friday and Saturday nights. My real weight (pre-weekend) is probably as much as five to eight pounds lighter. I have this weird knack for gaining weight extremely fast. It can take me four weeks to lose five pounds, yet I can easily put that back on in one bad night.

But I digress.

So here's the number: 206 pounds.

This is a slap in the face on so many levels. For starters, it's teasingly close to two hundred pounds. If I hadn't eaten so much over this past weekend, I might even be under two hundred. So close, but yet so far. There's a stigma associated with weighing in the two hundreds. The last time I weighed myself, back in June, I was 197.

I wish I were taller. I'm only five foot one. If I were, say, five foot eleven, 206 would not be so gargantuan.

I send Chelsea a quick e-mail relaying my "statistics." This probably sounds weird, but it's a habit we've had for the past two years. We try to weigh ourselves on a regular basis (the goal is once a week—although we usually end up doing it more like once a month) and then e-mail the info to each other.

It was Chelsea's idea to do this. She thinks it will help us keep our bodies in check. When you're unhappy with your weight, there's a tendency to steer clear of scales. The problem with this is you can easily balloon up without realizing it. Hence, what happened to me in fifth grade.

Chelsea is my height and weighs around 230 pounds. The scary thing is, this time last year, she weighed about 190. This is my worst nightmare. I'm not a big fan of my current body—but gaining forty pounds overnight would make the situation so much worse. I know this is awful, but I'm secretly glad that Chelsea weighs twenty-four pounds more than I do. When I'm with her, I don't have to be the biggest girl in the room. And that's nice.

I compose an e-mail to Chelsea. I tell her what Kimberlee and I have been up to (but I don't make it sound too fun—I don't want her to feel jealous) and I briefly mention a few Noah tidbits. Then I get to the real stuff.

> Sorry I haven't sent you any weight info since
> June. What can I say? I've been a bad girl. LOL!
> Then again, you can probably tell that, given
> my 9-pound gain. But you've been a bad girl
> too. I don't think you've sent me weight stats
> since May! ;) Get to it, missy! I know you've
> probably been pigging out on Spago's and
> California Pizza Kitchen for three months straight,
> but that's no excuse. It's time to face the music!
> And rest assured, once you get back to Atlanta
> (only two days!!!!), we can start hitting the gym
> every day after school and sharing oh-so-tasty
> Lean Cuisine meals for dinner. We'll nip this bitch
> in the bud, you can count on it!
> —Your BFFF (hopefully, minus one F soon!) Ryan
>
> PS Chad Michael Murray misses you!

I laugh as I read over the PS. A few years ago, Chelsea's mom got her a border collie for her birthday. At the time, Chelsea was head over heels in love with Chad Michael Murray, so she named her dog after him. A few months later, Chelsea came to her senses. I think it had something to do with the real Chad Michael Murray marrying Sophia Bush, then splitting with her mere weeks after their wedding. Or maybe she just realized what an overrated oaf he is.

At any rate, Chelsea has been trying to change her dog's name to Duke ever since, but no luck. No matter how hard she tries, her pup will only answer to Chad Michael Murray.

I always tease her about it, and she always pretends to get ticked off.

"Hey, it could be worse," I once pointed out. "At least you didn't name him James Van Der Beek."

Despite the cheery tone of my e-mail, I'm feeling a little down, so I decide to spend the afternoon hanging around the house.

When I first started taking Zoloft, I never thought there'd be days like this. I was seduced by the commercials with the little blob who is all sad and mopey before meds and happy and bouncy after them. I wanted to be like the bouncy blob.

I thought post-Zoloft life would be one big, long party—no pain, no heartache, just lots of happiness and fun. And in the beginning, it kind of was. Dr. Paige told me it could take up to six weeks to feel the effects of the medication, but I got them almost right away. I don't know if it was the placebo effect or not, but on the seventh day, I woke up feeling better than I had in a long, long time.

I'm a worrier by nature, but suddenly that stopped. All the stresses that normally plagued me seemed dim, far away, no longer so bad. I felt content, relaxed, okay with myself. Other pleasant things happened too. I stopped biting my nails, a habit I'd been trying to kick since I was six years old. I got more organized, especially when it came to cleaning my bedroom. In fact, I cleaned the whole house, come to think of it. In those first few weeks I had a seemingly endless supply of energy. I was doing things I'd never done before (at least not voluntarily): cleaning the oven, polishing the fine silver, alphabetizing my brother's massive CD collection.

But my Zoloft cheeriness didn't last forever. Before long, I was mellowing out, slipping back toward my normal self. I figured the problem was that I'd built up a tolerance, even though the packet insert swears that can't happen.

"Maybe we could up the dose?" I asked Dr. Paige.

"I don't think so," she said. "Fifty milligrams is the standard dose for someone your age."

*But what about for someone my weight?* I wanted to ask. But I didn't. I probably could have called Dr. Gibbons—he was the one who'd put me on it in the first place, after all—and asked to be bumped up, but I decided to leave it alone for the time being.

I have a lazy morning. I send Kimberlee a text message, wishing her a good first day of school. I'm glad I don't go to private, or I'd be in class today. Then again, they get longer fall and winter breaks than we do, so if you work it out, Kim actually has a shorter year than me.

The new e-mail icon flashes on my computer screen. I'm surprised to see that Chelsea has already written me back.

**From:** chels_bells89@hotmail.com (Chelsea Ramsay)

**To:** inthegutterlookingathestars@photo.lx (Ryan Burke)

**Sent:** Monday, August 28, 2006 10:27 AM

**Subject:** Re: Weight and stuff


I can't believe we haven't seen each other since May!
I didn't think I'd survive three months without you,
but Cali has been good to me. Even L.A., which I

thought would be the most superficial place on the planet (it is), has been fun.

Also, I hate to tell you in an e-mail, but I just found out today that I'm not coming back yet. Apparently, there was some miscommunication. My dad thought school didn't start back for another couple of weeks. Since he bought my ticket with frequent flyer miles, he's not going to be able to switch it. He was on the phone all morning with the airline, and then with the principal at Greenlee getting special permission for me to miss the first week or so of classes. It sucks. Sniff sniff. But my dad simply couldn't change the plane tickets. Something about blackout dates, I'm not sure. N-E-way, I'll be back in Hotlanta in no time.

Have fun in class without me and I'll see you soon!

—Chelsea, your BFFF (Best FAT Friend Forever . . . tee-hee!)

I can't believe she's not coming back on Wednesday. I've been looking forward to this all summer. I wish she'd called to tell me, but I figure she's busy hanging out with her dad and stuff.

Oh, well, nothing much to do, I guess. I find it odd that she doesn't mention my weight, but I figure she might be holding off to talk about it in person.

I head upstairs to wash my hair. I've just gotten out of the shower around eleven a.m. and I'm preparing to watch a *Beverly Hills, 90210* marathon on SOAPnet (I know that is so 1990, but I can't help it) when the phone rings. I glance at the caller ID. It's my grandfather's cell.

You know how most elderly people are clueless about technology? Not my granddad. He's sixty-eight, yet he's more up on Sidekicks, TiVo, and iPods than anyone my age.

"Want to do lunch today?" he asks. "I've got the afternoon off."

Every couple of months, my grandfather takes it upon himself to act like The Dad. I think he's always felt bad that Mark and I don't have a father figure in our lives, so he tries to fill in.

"I thought we could spend some time together before school starts back next week," he continues.

Normally I have a good excuse lined up when my grandpa calls. I tell him I've got homework, or that I'm volunteering at Habitat for Humanity (which I actually do, from time to time, though not nearly as often as my grandpa probably thinks), or that I'm going to the mall with Chelsea or something. It's not that I don't like spending time with him. I do—as long as other people are there to balance out the weirdness. Whenever we go out together, one-on-one, I wind up feeling awkward. Grandpa has a habit of bringing up the most disturbing topics imaginable. He's been known to discuss—in great detail— everything from his kidney stones to the latest episode of *The L Word*. All of this is easier to take when my mom and Mark are around, so I like having an excuse on hand when he asks me to hang out alone.

But today my mind goes blank. And since I don't think Grandpa will be too impressed that I'm planning to spend the day catching up with Brandon, Valerie, Dylan, and Kelly, I figure I might as well go.

"How about Brenneman's?" he asks.

I hate that place. The bread is always stale, the service always crappy. But what I say is, "I'll meet you there at noon."

For argument's sake, it is easier to go along. There are approximately three restaurants in town where my grandpa will eat. Everywhere else is "too unimaginative." Which is ironic, because my grandfather is a tax lawyer. Not exactly a field known for its creative minds.

"I can pick you up, if you want," he offers.

"Nah, Mark's home today. I can borrow his car." I'm hoping Grandpa will reply with something like, *Mark's there? Great! Bring him along!* But he doesn't.

Looks like it's just me and Gramps, for better or worse.

I hurriedly dry my hair and throw on a pair of Lane Bryant jeans and an Old Navy T-shirt (yes, Old Navy has shirts that fit me. I swear!) and head out the door. I even put on a little bit of makeup in the car (but only when I'm stopped at a light—I am a super safe driver, just so you know). I am looking pretty sharp, if I do say so myself. Which is why what Grandpa does during lunch completely throws me.

We're sitting there having turkey sandwiches and African peanut soup (which is Brenneman's specialty and which I actually love even though I am not usually a soup eater) when my grandfather slides this piece of paper across the table. "Here, I got this for you," he says between spoonfuls.

I stare down at the paper. It has the name ERICA KLOOS scrawled out, along with a phone number. I'm completely baffled. My first thought is that it's a business contact, perhaps the name of some photo editor who can help me get my foot in the door with an internship or something. But Grandpa squelches that right away by saying, "Erica is Rod

Pleedgrass's new secretary. She just started last month. I thought you two might enjoy talking. . . . You have a lot in common."

And I think, *Holy Christ, my Grandpa thinks I'm a lesbian!* My mind starts racing. I know *The L Word* is his favorite show, but come on! So I don't have a boyfriend. So I spend all my free time hanging out with girls. That doesn't mean I sleep with them! Why does he think this? Is it because I'm a photographer? Like, just because Annie Leibovitz is gay, I must be too? Oh God, in the "Junior Aspirations" section of last year's yearbook, I said my goal was to become the next Annie Leibovitz. Was that some kind of code that I was exiled in girlville, only I didn't know it?

This is beyond mortifying. I struggle to come up with a plan of attack. I debate saying something like, *You know, just because Robert Mapplethorpe is gay doesn't mean all photographers are.* Instead, I decide to take a laid-back approach.

"Grandpa, I don't really understand what you're getting at here."

"Erica just lost one hundred and twenty pounds on NutriSystem," he blurts out. "She's about to shoot one of their commercials. I've already spoken to her, and she said she'd be happy to help you."

Oh. My. God. As soon as he says that, our normal Monday afternoon lunch turns into a bad made-for-TV movie.

"What do you mean, 'help me'?"

"Help you deal with this weight problem of yours."

I choose my words carefully. "Why did you do this? Why did you go behind my back?" I ask, feeling my lower lip tremble. "Why didn't you ask me first?"

"Because you would have reacted exactly like you're reacting right now."

I don't say anything, merely stare down at my bowl of African peanut soup, which is getting cold.

"Ryan, I have always had your best interests in mind. That's the only thing I care about." He looks around the restaurant, seeming uncomfortable. "I want to give you opportunities to achieve more out of life, and I don't know that you can do that in your current state. We both know you have issues with your weight, and that it's going to pose a health risk for you."

"But I'm perfectly healthy!" I start to protest.

He holds up a hand to stop me. "Granted, right now, your health is not in any immediate danger. However, the older you get, the more serious this excess adipose tissue is going to become."

Adipose tissue? What the hell? Can't he just say "fat" and be done with it?

"It's going to put pressure on your heart. You're at risk for a whole host of serious ailments: hypertension, diabetes, high cholesterol, various types of cancer, among many, many other possibilities."

Like I don't know this stuff already. "I exercise," I say.

"Not enough."

I want to protest, but I know from past experience, it will get me nowhere. Trying to win an argument with a lawyer is damn near impossible.

"Now, why don't you get your chin up and finish your soup," he orders, dunking a piece of rock-hard bread into his bowl. "And first chance you get, call Erica."

I fold the piece of paper up and put it in my purse. Later, as we leave the restaurant, I throw it in the trash.

ARRIVE HOME TO FIND MY BROTHER IN A CLOUD OF smoke. He's sitting on the back porch, puffing away.

Pot, of course. It's always pot.

My brother is a major stoner. This is common knowledge to pretty much anyone who's ever met him. My mother knows about his drug habit—she *has* to—and she chooses to look the other way. My mom looks the other way on a lot of my brother's behavior.

When Mark got sick a few years ago, people stopped putting pressure on him. He didn't have to excel in school, clean his room, mow the lawn, play on the football team, take the PSATs. He could do his homework or not. Call his friends back or avoid them. Go to my grandparents' fortieth wedding anniversary or stay home.

Everyone cut him slack.

The only thing they expected him to do was get well and live.

As long as Mark was breathing, no one asked for more. No one wanted to push their luck.

And for a while, this made sense. When he was ill, he was *really* ill. As far as cancers go, childhood leukemia is more treatable than, say, a malignant brain tumor. If they catch it early, the chances for recovery are usually very good.

They did not catch Mark's cancer early.

It all went by in a blur—the bruises that didn't heal, the bleeding that wouldn't stop. One day he was a normal eighth grader—a running back for the Greenlee Junior High Cougars, Homecoming escort, treasurer of the SGA, captain of the Knowledge Bowl Team. You know, your typical Boy

Most Likely to. . . . The next thing we knew, he was fainting in football practice and vomiting blood in the back of my mother's car.

He had a girlfriend, Shelby, at the time. She broke up with him two days before he got sick. She wasn't being a bitch, it was just one of those freakish coincidences—the ultimate case of bad timing. Shelby was already dating someone else, a tenth grader named Elliot, when she heard the news about Mark. She immediately broke up with Elliot and asked Mark to take her back, which he did.

Shelby wanted to be there for Mark, to help him recover, and she did. She gave him something to fight for. Not that Mom and I weren't enough, but our family is small, and it was good to have someone else on the team, someone else rooting for Mark's recovery. Safety in numbers and all that.

Shelby fetched Mark's school assignments, sat by his hospital bed while he had chemo. And after chemo, when he was lying shivering on the bathroom floor, she fed him dry toast and ginger ale, then held his head steady while he brought them right back up.

The treatments made him horrifically ill. He lost a lot of weight and his hair, of course. We were on pins and needles, constantly waiting for any scrap of news, any change.

The chemo was working, then it wasn't, then it was again. That's the thing about chemotherapy. It's toxic. And in order for it to work, the doctors have to give you a dose that's just this side of lethal. They poison you until you're on the brink of death. Then they stop and hope it was enough, hope it killed the cancer.

Mark was sick for so long, and then, all of the sudden, he started getting better. His leukemia went into remission. But, as is the case with cancer, there's always the risk it will come back. Mark's never did, but we lived in fear for years, expecting a relapse, preparing for the worst.

After a while, we started to relax, but Mark didn't. From the outside he seemed the same. The casual observer wouldn't have noticed how much he'd changed, but I did. There were subtle differences. He broke up with Shelby, dropped his extracurriculars, quit thinking about college. He didn't want to make long-term plans. He was afraid to get too excited about anything. "Who cares about what happens tomorrow?" he told me once. "Life is to be lived right now, not in some perfect future time, not in some distorted memory of the past."

He was depressed, unhappy, nervous all the time. And then he found weed and never looked back.

"You want one?" he asks, offering me a blunt. This is a running joke between the two of us. He loves to pressure me to smoke with him, mainly because he knows I won't do it.

Whatever inkling I might have had to do drugs Mark killed long ago. I don't actually have a moral objection or anything. I've just seen the way Mark is. The way his entire life revolves around smoking weed.

I tried it with him—twice, actually—and nothing happened. I didn't get the munchies. Didn't get red eyes or mellow out or even feel paranoid. My mouth tasted awful, but other than that, it was completely uneventful. Mark thought it was hilarious.

"It doesn't affect some people," he told me. "I've only seen this once before, but they say as much as ten percent of the population can't get high off weed." He stared at me for a long, long time. "Damn," he finally whispered. "You don't know what you're missing."

Again, I blame the sperm bank. I bet my father passed along the pot-doesn't-affect-me gene.

It's not that I want to get high all the time or anything. But it's annoying that there's this supposedly great experience out there and I'm immune to it. I feel like one of those women who've never had an orgasm before. They go through life never understanding what the big fuss is about.

Then again, maybe I'm lucky. I'd hate to live like Mark. His day is always the same. Wake up, smoke pot. Go to work at a shitty job as a Walgreens checker—spend eight hours thinking about smoking pot. Take lunch break, smoke pot. Get off work, smoke pot. He's twenty years old, and a day does not pass that he isn't high. He's completely obsessed with the stuff. They say it's not addictive, but then they say the same thing about food. And God knows I'm powerless over things like Doritos and cheesecake.

"Ryan," he says, nodding his head slightly as he sees me. "Got somethin' for you."

"Oh?"

He slowly gets up, makes his way inside the house. "A message. From Dave or Dan or Doug. Something like that. I thought I wrote this down, but now I can't find the paper." He snaps his fingers. "Ben . . . Benjamin."

"Benjamin." My heart starts racing. "Benjamin McGann?"

"I think so."

Benjamin McGann is a big-name photographer from New York. He's known for taking slice-of-life Americana shots. Benjamin is temporarily living in Atlanta—the rumor is his mother's ill and he's down here to look after her. While he's in town he's going to be running a twelve-week seminar/ workshop for up-and-coming photographers. It's only open to high school students, and everyone who's anyone is dying to get in. I sent in my portfolio and application last month, but I haven't heard back. I'd all but lost hope that I'd land a slot. But surely Benjamin McGann wouldn't call personally to reject me.

"Oh, my God! Did you get the number?"

"Yeah. It's on the paper. Which seems to have disappeared."

"Mark!" I thunder. "This is really, really important."

"What's really important?" Mom asks, sidling up to me. I didn't hear her come in.

"Benjamin McGann called earlier today, and this idiot lost the message!"

There's a moment of silence as it dawns on Mom exactly what this means. "Mark!" she scolds him. "I've told you this a thousand times. If you're not going to take a coherent message, then don't answer the phone. We have voice mail for a reason." She turns to face me. "Do you have a way to get in touch with him?"

"No," I sniffle. I'm in complete shock. I start tearing through the house, desperate to find my paperwork on the program. If nothing else, I can call the university where the class is being held and see if someone there knows how to get in touch with him.

I'm on my mad rampage when Mark calls out, "Found it."

"Well, thank God for that!" I say, running back into the kitchen. I grab the piece of paper from his hands and pick up the cordless. With shaking hands, I dial the number.

"Benjamin McGann," a high-pitched voice says.

I'm thrown off. "Hi, Mr. McGann," I begin.

"This is his assistant, Becca."

"Um, yes, Ms., um, Becca." Wow, I'm an idiot when I'm nervous. "I received a message from Mr. McGann asking me to call him."

"And this is in regards to . . . ?"

"The young photographers' workshop."

"And your name is . . . ?"

"Ryan Burke."

"Right. Hold, please." She's gone for what seems like forever but is probably no more than two minutes. "He just wanted to inform you that you've been accepted to the course."

"I have!" I shriek, unable to keep my cool.

"Yes. The first session is Saturday, September sixteenth, at seven a.m. sharp," she says. "You'll need to bring two rolls of unprocessed film. You can take photos of whatever you'd like, just make sure they're black-and-white. You won't do color until the second half of the term, and you'll need to use C41-compliant film for that. You'll get a packet in the mail explaining all of this." She goes on to give me directions to the classroom, and then we hang up.

I'm so excited, I can barely speak. Mom comes back into the kitchen and we hug.

"I got in, I got in!" I scream.

"I heard!" she says, squeezing me tightly. "I'm so excited!"

Mark pokes his head around the corner. "Something goin' on?"

"Ryan made the photography class!" Mom says, beaming proudly.

"Well," Mark says, shrugging his shoulders, in an *I couldn't care less* gesture, "whoopty freaking do." He stops for a minute, then says, "I bet this class is expensive."

He's right. "It's not cheap," I tell him.

"How is she getting the money?" he asks Mom.

"Your grandparents have agreed to help out since they know how important this is," Mom says.

At the mention of Grandpa, my mood sinks again. I want to push the awful lunch as far from my mind as possible.

"Damn it!" Mark says. "I should have gone to lunch with Grandpa today. I could have kissed his ass and maybe he would have bought me a new car."

"That's not why your sister had lunch with your grandfather," Mom says. "This was decided weeks ago, back when Ryan first applied."

I wonder how she knows about the lunch since I didn't tell her. I guess Grandpa must have called her afterward to fill her in on the Erica Kloos situation. Ugh.

"I'm sure if you'd like to take a class," Mom continues, "at one of the local community colleges or something, your grandparents would be happy to help out."

"No thanks," Mark says. "I'm not wasting my time on those crappy schools." He rolls his eyes and stalks out the room.

I hate the way he talks to Mom; I hate that she lets him. But it's like I said. Ever since his sickness, no one expects anything of Mark. It used to depress me. I wanted to shout at them, shake my mom and grandparents by the shoulders and say, *You think you're helping him, but you're not! He's got all this potential and he's wasting it! You're encouraging him to waste it!*

But then I thought about it one day, and I realized

something: How did I know? How did I *truly* know Mark wasn't living up to his potential? How did I know this wasn't exactly how his life was supposed to turn out? We all want to believe we're destined for greatness, but the truth is, we're probably not. There isn't even enough "greatness" to go around.

There are 6 billion people in the world. It would only make sense, mathematically, that most of us are meant for mediocrity. Most of us aren't meant to change the world in any substantial way. We're just meant to live our lives, for however long we've got them, and then slip into obscurity when we die. Maybe Mark is supposed to be a checker at Walgreens for the rest of his life. Maybe that's how he's supposed to spend the next forty years. Maybe that's all there is for him.

For a lot of people, that's all there is.

It's times like this when I start thinking, *Screw fifty!* Even a thousand milligrams of Zoloft wouldn't do.

### MISCONCEPTIONS/THINGS
### I WISH PEOPLE KNEW ABOUT ME

*I do not eat fifteen hamburgers in one sitting.*
*I eat a lot less than most people think.*

*I am very active. I love (okay, like) working*
  *out. Sort of.*
*Losing weight is not half as easy as you*
  *think it is.*
*I'm not lazy.*
*I'm not boring.*
*I'm not desperate.*
*I don't stuff my face all day long.*
*I am not a slut.*
*I'm not frigid.*
*I do not get out of breath walking across*
  *the room.*
*I'm not like some fat character you see*
  *in a movie.*
*I do not have a bad personality/attitude.*
*You don't know me half as well as you*
  *think you do.*

# Freudian Slips

## DR. PAIGE NORRIS, PhD, MD

PATIENT: *Ryan Burke*

PERSONAL GOALS FOR THE WEEK

1. *Stop obsessing over ex-boyfriends and move on. Accomplish this by making a date with someone new and exciting.*

# Chapter Three

THE FIRST DAY OF SCHOOL ALWAYS SUCKS. THERE'S nothing worse than having to get back to the daily grind when you've been sleeping late for the past three months.

Although it's not like I was a total slacker. I was working at the DigiHut four days a week, so it's not like I stayed in bed until noon.

Still, I don't want to be here.

The big news around campus is that Max Steadman's party has been postponed indefinitely. He got busted for DUI over the weekend, so he's got to keep a low profile or risk winding up in juvie. Everyone in homeroom is buzzing about it. The story is interesting at first, but I grow bored listening to it over and over again.

I read Chelsea's latest e-mail over while I wait for the first bell to ring.

**From:** chels_bells89@hotmail.com (Chelsea Ramsay)

**To:** inthegutterlookingathestars@photo.lx (Ryan Burke)

**Sent**: Sunday, September 3, 2006 9:52 PM

**Subject:** Hell-A

I saw Nicky Hilton at a club last night. Nicky freaking Hilton! I wish it had been Paris, even though I hate that girl with every fiber in my being. What was I doing at a club, you ask? Other than sharing body shots with the hottest Latino boy this side of Miami? It's a long story. One that involves a fake ID, a drug mule, and four million dollars' worth of diamonds. Now, if that doesn't sound like a plot to the latest Jerry Bruckheimer movie, I don't know what does! I'll have to tell you all the details when I get home. Just another week, baby! Have a great first day of school! Tell everyone I said hi. I'll be thinking about you.

—Chelsea (aka your tequila lovin' friend)

PS I feel bad for not telling you about this sooner, but it's a sensitive subject and I didn't want to bring it up. I kind of don't want to do our weight

sharing thing anymore.

PPS (Or is it PSS—I can never remember!) There's

a giant billboard of Noah on the Sunset Strip.

Totally surreal!

I printed it out last night and I've read it over about a dozen times. At first it really freaked me out, but I've come to a conclusion. The e-mail is either a complete and total joke, or Chelsea is on drugs.

And, given her aversion to all things narc-related, it's got to be the former.

Before she left for California, Chelsea was the most low-key, laid-back person you could ever hope to meet. Her idea of a good time was ordering a pizza and watching a DVD of *Friends*. She didn't like crowds. Didn't like parties. Didn't want anything to do with drugs or alcohol or clubs.

Also, and I'm not trying to be mean here, but Chelsea's kind of big. Really big. Bigger-than-me big. And it's not like I know the L.A. club scene well, or even the Atlanta one for that matter, but I kind of always figured you had to be slim and glamorous to make it past the velvet rope.

She must have made the story up, just to see if I was paying attention.

Which I definitely was. Her PS (both of them) kind of depressed me. She must have been disappointed when I e-mailed her about my nine-pound weight gain. Hell, I'm disappointed.

I mean, I had this whole master plan: With the help of a strict low-carb diet and rigorous exercise regime, I was going to shed a cool fifty pounds in the time span between May and August. Fifty pounds in three months is not unrealistic. It's not easy, but it's certainly doable. I think someone on *The Biggest Loser* lost, like, eighty pounds in that time span. And he was a lot older than I am. I'm young. I should have a fast(ish) metabolism.

But I guess I spent too much time indoors, working behind the counter at DigiHut. There were always snacks around, and Kimberlee did daily coffee runs. Come to think of it, I did drink a lot of Frappuccinos this summer. And I ate a lot of Starbucks cookies and my fair share of Burger King fried-chicken sandwiches.

But in my own defense I also downed a lot of bottled waters, Jared-approved Subway sandwiches, and fat-free Dannon yogurts. It's weird the way it adds up in your mind.

When it comes to losing weight, you absolutely cannot trust your memory. You never log things accurately—it always feels like you ate better and exercised more than you actually did.

My recollection of eating the boring foods is so vivid—choking down celery sticks, suffering through cups of low-sodium veggie soup—that it feels like I must have eaten that way 24/7. But it was probably only half the time, at best.

I also remember exercising all the damn time. I remember buying that light blue tracksuit at Lane Bryant back in May. And I remember picking up a new pair of SKECHERS and uploading a ton of Mark's CDs to my iPod. I even remember hitting the gym a bunch of times. It felt like I was going four or five days a week, but it was probably closer to one or two.

This is what I hate about losing weight. It takes approximately a billion years to see results. If I ate a lean meal and then dropped a dress size overnight, I could stick to it so much better. But that's not how it works. You eat right over and over and over again, and then you (maybe) see some results.

Sigh.

I can't dwell on this right now. I have too much else on my

mind. Like how to make my senior year the best year ever! Not to get all cheesy and *Rah! Rah! Rah!* school-spirited, but this is the big one. This is my last chance to make high school actually count for something, and I'll be damned if I'm going to let it slip away.

My first couple of classes are boring. Physics, Latin, precalculus. After that, I've got lunch. I meet up with Delia McConnelly, one of my best "school friends." With Chelsea gone, Delia is my closest pal at Greenlee. A little sad, if you think about it. Delia and I have eaten lunch together for four years. We've sat together at pep rallies and football games, even gone to the mall a bunch of times. Yet, I still feel guarded around her. I don't talk to her, or tell her private things like I do with Chelsea. Or even Kimberlee.

I follow Delia over to the popular table. We always sit at the popular table.

I know this probably sounds weird—a contradiction, even. Because fat girls are supposed to be unpopular geeks, right? At least, that's the way we're always portrayed in the movies. We're usually shown as the big losers who eat lunch (an enormously big lunch, it often seems) by ourselves. I hate this, because it's so not true. Fat girls can be popular; fat girls can have lots of friends. Where we sometimes strike out is with boyfriends. That area's a little harder to breach. But none of the girls in school have ever ignored me for being overweight.

There's a new girl sitting at our table. Her name's Shady and she's from Miami. Shady wastes no time telling us that Atlanta is utterly boring. "Your club scene here sucks," she says.

Delia already sort of knows Shady. They met this morning in Spanish class. As we sit down, Delia introduces me as "the girl who used to date Noah Fairbanks!" and Shady squeals and gets really excited. Now that the subject has been broached, we spend almost the entire lunch period talking about him. Noah is big news at our school, and everyone wants the inside scoop. Shady, especially, has a million questions. I'm used to this. I've been getting them for years:

*Was he a good kisser? Did you ever talk about getting married? Does he still think about you? How much money did Noah really earn last year? Because* Us Weekly *said it was $4 million, and* Rolling Stone *said $11. Not that it matters— it's a lot of money, no matter how you look at it—but it would be nice to know. Is he dating Lindsay Lohan? Because I saw a picture of them together in* People *and they looked super tight. Then again, the* New York Post *has him with Ashlee Simpson, so maybe Noah's seeing her. When's the next* *time he's coming back to Atlanta, and will he stop by the school and say hi to everyone? Will he perform at our Homecoming dance? He really should, because this is his alma matter, his legacy. Are you going to ask him to prom? You should call his mother and get the scoop on what he's up to now. You must have gotten close to his family, right?*

I have achieved a pretty big level of fame at Greenlee High, thanks to my ex. I can't decide if this is a good or bad thing. In truth, it's nice to be known for something, but part of me feels weird being connected to Noah's success. Because I'm not.

The conversation is fun at first, but pretty soon my old paranoia sets in. I feel like I'm living this weird existence, stuck in the past, clinging to a guy I'll never have again.

It's like Chelsea said: I don't want to wind up like my mother. Not to sound like a bitch, but that is one of my greatest fears. My mother is practically asexual. She does not date. Ever. I haven't seen her with a man since I was really young. I know she had a boyfriend once, a serious one, when she was in grad school.

His name was Bill and, from what I gather, he broke her heart in about ten thousand pieces. Then he ran it over with an eighteen-wheeler and doused it with gasoline for good measure.

He was the one who got away, the perfect guy she thought she couldn't live without.

And she was right. She didn't live without him, not really. Once their relationship was over, *all* of her relationships were over. I guess if she couldn't have Bill, then she didn't want anyone.

As Shady drones on and on about Noah, I start to panic.

I'm losing myself. My personality's slipping, sliding right off the page. I have dissolved somewhere in a sea of Noah Fairbanks. The most interesting thing about me isn't even about me.

Lately, I've been thinking about Noah constantly, having these stupid fantasies about him. Mostly they involve him flying into Atlanta, showing up on my doorstep, and telling me that he can't live without me. Then I drop out of school and join him on the road.

We have this crazy passionate relationship. It's wild and sex-fueled, and we can't keep our hands off each other (which is the polar opposite of how things were, back in the day). And, of course, I'm thin in these fantasies. Noah Fairbanks, Rock Star, cannot have a fat girlfriend.

It's silly, actually, because I never felt this way when he first became famous. As amazing as it may seem, I didn't want him back. Even though he was new and improved (courtesy of a record-company makeover) and even though he was rich, I didn't pine for him. I knew that our time had passed, and I knew that we weren't meant to be.

And I guess I know that now, too. That's why I won't pick up the phone and call him. If I really believed we were meant to be together, I would do that, right?

The rest of the afternoon goes by quickly. After lunch I have English, then study hall. My last class of the day is history. I'm running late, so I rush in the door and nearly smack into Josh Lancaster.

"Sorry," I say, jumping out of his way.

"No prob," he says, scurrying out into the hall to give his girlfriend, Megan, a quick kiss before class starts.

Josh and I have this strange relationship. Or nonrelationship, as the case may be.

Josh Lancaster is, quite literally, the boy next door. Up until the age of ten, Josh and I were best friends. We spent every waking moment together—playing Xbox, watching *The Lion King*, challenging each other to badminton matches. Our parents used to have this running joke that one day we'd grow up and get married. But then Josh got hot, and I got fat, and nobody said that anymore. People never talk about the fat girl and the hot guy winding up together because, sadly, it just doesn't happen.

Still, it would be nice if Josh and I could be friends. As it is, he doesn't even acknowledge my existence.

Oh, well. As I'm finding out, friendships that existed in the past tend to stay there.

'M DYING TO TALK TO CHELSEA. HER LATEST E-MAIL really freaked me out, and I want to get the scoop.

Unfortunately, though, she seems too busy to talk to me. The entire first week of school passes and I don't hear back from her.

I send two texts, an e-mail, and leave numerous phone messages. Finally, around eleven o'clock on Thursday, Chelsea calls.

"You're obsessing again," she says when I answer the phone.

"No, I'm not."

"Yes, you are." She laughs. "Why else would you blow up my phone like that?"

"I just wondered how you were," I say. "You're my best friend and I've barely talked to you during the past two weeks. All summer, actually. And your last e-mail was so strange! What was I supposed to think?"

Chelsea giggles. "I thought that might get your attention."

I ask her to fill me in, and she does. Despite my prediction, it turns out the story is, in fact, true. The fake ID is hers, procured from a seedy stall she ran across while shopping in Venice Beach.

"It cost fifty bucks," Chelsea tells me, "but it was so worth it! Now I'm twenty-one instead of seventeen!"

She doesn't tell me how, as a fat girl, she got into the club, and I don't ask. Sensitive subject, you understand.

"I'm telling you, Ryan, tequila is the greatest thing ever invented." Chelsea laughs. "Once I started drinking it, I became totally outgoing, not self-conscious at all. You should try it sometime!"

I resent the tone of her voice; it's condescending, like she knows something I don't, has experienced something I haven't. Although, in a way, she has. I listen, with interest, to the rest of the story.

The Latino boy was someone she ran into at the club and, yes, the body shots actually happened.

"I can't believe I did a thing like that!" She giggles. "He had his tongue inches from my belly button. It was so strange. It tickled. Afterward, we made out in the back of his friend's car for almost an hour."

I'm shocked. This is the most Chelsea has done with a guy, at least as far as I know. Before she left Atlanta she was more virginal than me.

The diamonds and drug mules portions of the story are the only things that are slightly embellished.

"Miguel, that's the body-shot boy's name, is trying to get into movies. He's mostly a walk-on right now, but he wants to do more."

Walk-ons, Chelsea tells me, are nonspeaking actors on films. Basically, he's one of those extras you see in the background, taking up space at a nearby table so the leading man and lady don't have to sit in an empty restaurant.

"Miguel's working with an acting coach and a diction coach," she goes on. "He has a big audition for a bit part in an action movie this week, so I helped him run lines."

"Was this before or after he licked tequila off your stomach?"

"After." She giggles. "And you don't lick the tequila—you lick the salt."

"I see."

"The scene was so stupid. Miguel has to play a drug mule who tries to steal four million dollars' worth of jewelry from the coke dealer's wife and winds up getting shot."

"What a splendid role." I mean it as a joke, but it comes out sounding sarcastic.

"He didn't really want to go out for it. He doesn't like being stereotyped as a Latino. He says all the roles he's up for are so 'token Hispanic guy,' it's pathetic."

There's an awkward silence for a minute. Now that Chelsea is finished with her story, neither of us really knows what to say. I feel so disconnected from her. She's out in L.A. doing the kinds of crazy things we used to only talk about.

"So it sounds like you guys really connected," I say. "Are you going to see him again?"

"I doubt it. Why would I? One and done, baby, one and done!"

"One and done?"

"One night, then you take flight. I learned it from Javier."

"Who?"

"Miguel's brother."

"You met his brother?"

"Uh-huh. When we went back to his apartment."

"You went to this strange guy's apartment?!" I can barely believe what she's saying. "What did your dad think of all this?"

"Oh, please, like he knows. I lied and said I was going to

a late movie." She laughs. "Anyway, how have you been?"

I fill her in on the Benjamin McGann photography class and she's psyched for me.

"There's not a lot else going on in my life at the moment. Do you know when you're coming back?"

"No . . ."

"But you've already missed four days of classes! Everyone's piling on work already. Mr. Miller"—that's the twelfth-grade English teacher—"already assigned a huge paper on comparing and contrasting *Hamlet* and *Macbeth*. You're going to have to come back soon or you'll be way behind."

"I know." Her voice sounds flat. "But there's not much I can do about it. It's not my decision."

"Well, when is your return ticket booked for?"

"I'm not sure. . . . We're still sorting that out. As soon as I know something, you'll be the first person I'll call."

"Yeah, right. 'Cause you've been so good about calling lately and all," I snap, without meaning to.

She pauses for a minute. "I know. I'm sorry. I've been pretty distant. Despite all the fun I'm having, things out here are . . . weird. I don't mean to give you the cold shoulder. I've been having a kind of rough time of it, truth be told."

"Dad problems?" I blurt, without thinking. I instantly feel bad. Chelsea's life is one big dad problem. Her relationship with her father is so bad, it almost makes me grateful to be a sperm-bank baby. Almost.

"Yeah . . ." Her voice trails off.

"What's going on?"

"The usual," she says, and I get the sense she doesn't want to talk about it.

The usual typically means one of two things: Either Chelsea's dad has a new girlfriend—probably someone twenty-two and blond with fake tits—or he's ragging her about her weight again. It's awful, but Chelsea's father has never accepted the fact that she's fat. He seems horrified by it—offended, even.

I remember when we were younger and he still lived in Atlanta. Chelsea used to spend every weekend at his apartment—a dingy loft downtown—and she'd always beg me to go along with her. Most of the time I said no, but every now and again, I felt sorry and caved in.

It was a guaranteed bad time, and I hated seeing how stressed out she got going over there.

Her father's place was the pits. No privacy. Nothing fun to do. The man didn't believe in "letting children rot their brains by watching TV," so he'd unhook the cable.

The only music he allowed us to listen to was Mozart or Beethoven. But those weren't the bad parts. The bad part was the way he would desperately try to control Chelsea's eating. He'd dole out portions for her as though she were a toddler—little spoonfuls of mushy peas and carrots, a palm-size portion of lean chicken without the skin.

He would constantly criticize her eating habits and threaten to send her to fat camp if she didn't shape up. It was awful.

"You eat like you're trying to fatten yourself up on purpose," he joked once, pointing at her thigh. "You're not a Christmas ham."

He talked to her like that a lot. And she rarely ever reacted, rarely got upset. Which led me to conclude that either she was so used to hearing him speak this way that it no longer fazed her, or that she was burying her emotions, too ashamed to let anyone see how wounded she was.

One weekend, Chelsea and her dad got into a huge fight right in front of me. It started when Chels complained that she needed to watch the DVD of *The Hours* for English class. Her dad refused to allow it.

"I find it very hard to believe," her father had scoffed, "that your English teacher would force you to watch a movie as homework. I thought the purpose of that class was to diagram sentences."

"We haven't done that since seventh grade," she pointed out. "We're studying Virginia Woolf right now, and—"

"Virginia Woolf was a writer," he said, cutting her off.

"I know that, Dad—"

"Then shouldn't you be reading her work, rather than watching the film version? Honestly, Chelsea, you're so fucking lazy. I know you'd rather keep your fat ass bolted to the seat than actually get up and move it around; I get that. I get that you're a couch potato. I get that you would rather watch TV than play racquetball or go for a jog around the block."

I'd stood there for a moment, shocked to hear him talk to her like that. It was the first time I'd heard him call her fat, and it upset me. He was always trying to get her to exercise, always begging her to eat the way he wanted her to. But somehow the words were so much worse.

"We just finished reading *Mrs. Dalloway*," I piped up. "We were supposed to watch *The Hours* so we could get a better idea of her life and of how the novel affected people."

He ignored me. "*The Hours*," he repeated, thinking it over. A weird look appeared on his face. "Isn't that a dyke movie?"

"Yeah, kind of. But that's not really the point," Chelsea said.

He picked the DVD up off the table. "You tell your teacher you're not allowed to watch this kind of trash."

I never spent the night over there again.

A few months later Chelsea's dad got into a major car accident. He didn't have any serious long-term damage, but it took several months of physical therapy and a minor knee operation before he was okay again. Fortunately (or unfortunately, depending on how you look at it), the driver of the other vehicle—a delivery truck for a major carrier—was drunk at the time. A quick out-of-court settlement later, and Chelsea's dad was able to quit his job, move across the country, and open a surf shop. I've always kind of thought his leaving was the best thing that could have happened to Chels. Now she doesn't have to deal with his constant ridicule. Plus, no more weekly visits to his hellish apartment.

"Dad just started dating this new girl," Chelsea says, snapping me back to the present. "She's a wannabe actress and she's only twenty-five. Here's the worst part. Her name is"—she pauses for dramatic effect—"Tidal."

"Title?" I ask, not sure I've heard it right.

"No. Tidal. T-I-D-A-L," she spells it out for me. "She's

awful, Ryan. She lies around the house all day, painting her toenails and watching TV."

"Your dad lets her watch TV?" I ask, surprised. "I thought he used to hate it."

"Tidal's not fat," she explains. "I think Dad hated me watching TV because he thought that's what was keeping me overweight. He figured I should be out and about, revving up my metabolism instead of sitting on the couch like a sloth."

I kind of guessed as much, but I don't say anything.

"So you're stuck there with her all day?"

"Yes!" She sighs. "It's horrible. She's supposed to be going on auditions, but she never leaves the house. At least she hasn't moved in yet. Although most nights she sleeps over." Chelsea pauses, then lowers her voice. "It's so gross, Ryan. I can, like, hear them having sex through the walls at night!"

I take a minute to process this disgusting tidbit.

"Okay, I'm not trying to be an ass . . . but why on earth did you agree to go out there for the summer?" It's the question I've been asking her, over and over again, since she abruptly decided to leave last June.

"Because I never see my dad anymore."

"I thought that was a good thing."

"Hey! He's my father, all right. Chill," she says, sounding offended. And then I remember the family double-standard rule. It's okay for her to talk about what a dick her dad is, but that's off-limits for me. We talk for a while longer, then we hang up the phone.

# Freudian Slips

## DR. PAIGE NORRIS, PhD, MD

PATIENT: *Ryan Burke*

PERSONAL GOALS FOR THE WEEK

1. Stop obsessing over ex-boyfriends and move on. Accomplish this by making a date with someone new and exciting. (This goal is repeated, since you failed to do it last week!)

2. Try something you swore you'd never do.

# Chapter Four

I LIKE HAVING A FRIEND WHO'S KIND OF A SLUT.

It opens you up to new experiences, things you wouldn't be exposed to otherwise. Since I started hanging around with Kimberlee last May, I've been privy to all sorts of strange stuff.

Like when I walked in on her having sex with a customer in the break room at DigiHut (which wouldn't have been so shocking if, two days before, I hadn't walked in on her having sex with the assistant manager in the break room at DigiHut).

I know people think it's crazy that I want to hang around someone like this, especially considering I'm so inexperienced myself. But then I guess that's why I like it. I get to live vicariously through Kim, stand back while she does all the things I'd never have the nerve to do (and probably wouldn't want to do, anyway).

The truth is, my own dating life has been a miserable mess. Other than Noah, there have only been two guys.

And they are . . .


**Name:** Kirby. I swear to God, I can't even remember his last name.

**Dated:** Four weeks. Yes, a measly four weeks.

**The vital stats:** We met at a photography course during the summer after tenth grade. Kirby was older than me by eight years. Only I didn't know it at the time. He lied about his age, telling me he was nineteen when he was actually twenty-four. He was a photography student at a nearby college (I thought he was a sophomore; he was actually a grad assistant) and he was teaching photography to high school students to beef up his résumé. The class was really basic: how to use light meters, mixing chemicals in a darkroom, the best exposure time for a print. I already knew those kinds of things, so Kirby offered to give me extra, outside-the-classroom instruction so I wouldn't be bored. God, I was so naive. Being with a nice guy like Noah did nothing to prepare me for the nightmare that was Kirby.

**I love yous:** No. Hell no!!!!

**Sex:** Okay, this one's kind of embarrassing. It all started because Kirby and I used to get drunk together in the evenings. We'd go out shooting photos until the light got too dim, and then we'd head back to his apartment and make out. He'd serve me shots of Grey Goose and Red Bull while we'd watch episodes of his favorite shows, *Entourage* and *Arrested Development*. It was all really fun and exciting (I felt like such a badass, sneaking around, hooking up with a college guy) until he tried to take things too far.

I'd confessed on the front end that I was a virgin. A humiliating confession, but I wanted to be honest. Plus, I was sloshed the day I told him. So when he started taking off my clothes one night, I protested. I was feeling dizzy—from the booze, from being alone with him—and he kept kissing me, gently, saying, "I know you're not going to go there. I can respect that. But there are other things we can do." I was nervous and scared, and I didn't want him to see me naked because I felt so fat.

But I gave in.

Next thing I knew, my shirt was undone and his mouth was on me. And then he moved lower, down to my stomach, and I held my breath, trying to make myself look thinner. He kissed my stomach for a while. God knows why. I wasn't pancake-flat like Kimberlee or any of the other millions of skinny girls, and I couldn't see how my squishy flesh could turn him on. But he kept at it, kissing and kissing, inching lower and lower. And then, all of the sudden, he was going down on me and the room was spinning and I kept staring over at the TV, watching Vincent Chase make out with Mandy Moore and trying not to scream.

He knew what he was doing. *Oh God, did he know.*

It was a strange and (I'm not going to lie) nice experience.

Very, *very* nice.

"I've never felt this good in my life!" Nice, if you want to get technical.

What was not so nice was when, the next day, Kirby expected me to give in and sleep with him. And when I wouldn't do that, he grabbed my head and tried to force it down. "I'm just not . . . I'm not comfortable doing that yet. . . ." I'd left it open-ended. I was nervous about going there, even though most of my friends had been giving blow jobs for years and none of them even considered it a big deal. But still, I hadn't done it before, not to Noah, not to anyone, and I had to work up my nerve. I asked him to give me some time, a few weeks maybe, and then I'd try.

Kirby was not impressed. "Man, what a fucking waste of time!" he growled, jumping up off the couch. "I spend all this fucking money buying you vodka all summer and then I waste forty-five minutes giving you my best action and you won't even return the favor? What a bitch!"

He drove me home, grumbling the entire way about what a cocktease I was. And when he dropped me off, he said it, the thing that stopped me cold, rendered me powerless. The one thing for which I had no comeback.

He made a fat comment.

Tilting his head back and laughing, he shouted, "I can't believe I wasted this much time on a fat girl! I hate fat girls!" as he slammed the door behind me. I stood there, dumbfounded, on the sidewalk in front of my house, and watched him drive off down the street.

**Degree my <u>fat</u> hindered the relationship, on a scale of 1 to 10: 10? 1?** Who knows. He might have been saying it out of spite. Probably not.

**Name:** Ryan Andrew Sully (Yes, I dated a guy named Ryan. After two weeks of confusion, we decided I would call him Andrew. See, once again, my mother's stupid "You're a sperm-bank baby, so it doesn't matter if I give you a boy's name" theory has come back to bite me in the ass.)

**Dated:** Five months; broke up over spring break of my junior year.

**The vital stats:** After the Kirby fiasco, I decided to date only pure, wait-until-marriage guys who wouldn't pressure me in any way. I met Andrew at a church carnival Chelsea's cousin took us to. He was cute and sweet, and he said he thought I had a "really pretty face." He used to give me this compliment on a daily basis, only he'd switch it up, so that sometimes it was "lovely face" or "beautiful face" instead of just "pretty." I know he didn't mean it this way, but it stung like a backhanded compliment. Couldn't he have just said I was pretty and left it at that?

In the end, it was my weight that did us in. My attitude about my weight, that is.

Andrew was so sweet and understanding—he wanted to grow up to be a grief counselor, for God's sake—and he made you feel like you could talk to him about anything. So I did. I talked and talked and talked. I told him about gaining weight at ten, and how I thought it might be linked to my brother's illness. I told him about the pains of finding clothes that fit, about how every time I stepped on the scale I wanted to die. I recounted my fantasies of being thin, of all the diets I'd tried. I complained about the Weight Watchers Points

System, the South Beach cookbook, the Lean Cuisine frozen dinners I choked down most nights. I told him about all of my cravings. How I would give my right arm for a brownie or a bowl of mac and cheese.

"It's not your actual weight. Your weight doesn't bother me," Andrew said. "But it bothers *you* so much. You're neurotic about it, completely obsessed. I hope someday you'll see you the way I see you. But for now, this isn't working. I just can't take it anymore. I'm sorry."

**I love yous:** We said it on Valentine's Day, and it was kind of sweet.

**Sex:** Not even close.

**Degree my <u>fat</u> hindered the relationship, on a scale of 1 to 10:** 10.


I'm discouraged by how much my fat has affected all of my relationships. But, never mind! That's the past and, like Dr. Paige says, I've got to start looking toward the future.

And the future . . . is men.

Fortunately, Kimberlee seems ready to help me out on that front. The following Friday night we go to the movies to see *The Covenant*. The film opened at number one last weekend, but tonight the theater's virtually deserted. (The movie industry just can't catch a break these days.) We take seats on the far-left-hand side, a good five rows from anybody. It works out well, since *The Covenant* is dumb and we end up talking the entire time.

During a stupid part where one of the male leads is trying to harness his supernatural powers, Kim leans over and hisses in my ear, "I found you a guy for tomorrow!"

"A guy?" I say, startled. What is she talking about? I haven't asked her to set me up with anyone. I panic briefly as I remember her plan to hook up with guys online. Fortunately, she seems to have forgotten about that.

"Yeah. His name's Dave. He's going to a party tomorrow and he wants to take someone. I told him you'd be perfect."

The guy on the screen is trying, and failing, to act like a warlock. I turn toward her. "I don't know about this. Isn't it short notice? It'll look bad if I accept a date with him at the last minute, won't it? Like I'm so pathetic, I've got nothing better to do."

"Don't worry about that." Kim waves her hand dismissively. "Dave's a great guy, and this is a great opportunity. Don't pass it up. Besides"—she giggles—"he's an awesome kisser."

"How do you know that?"

"I tested him out! He's also got an enormous dick."

This is kind of gross that she knows that, but I don't say anything. "Uh . . . okay. Maybe I could go out with him."

"You've got to! A party sounds fun."

It sounds scary, but I don't tell her this. I'm more terrified of a date with Dave than I am of the horror movie we're watching. I know what Kim's guy friends are like. As far as I can tell, she's slept with most of them.

"He's kind of a man ho," she says, confirming my suspicions. "But right about now, I think that's what you need."

"How much of a man ho are we talking about here?" I ask, nervously chewing on my lower lip.

"Uh . . . not sure."

"How many girls has he slept with?"

"You really want to know that?"

"I asked."

Kim sighs. "I don't know, thirty. Fifty. Maybe more. He was in a band a few years ago. I think he got a lot of play back then." Seeing my stricken expression, she quickly adds, "But don't worry! Dave would never try to force you to do something you don't want to do. Never, I swear. If he did, I'd beat his ass." She laughs, but I'm still feeling unsure.

91

"Are you sure he wants to go out with me?" Again, my insecurity is rearing its ugly head. I should be asking, "Are you sure I want to go out with him?" but I don't think this way. In my own mind, I am always the underdog.

"Yeah! I totally showed him a picture. An accurate one, too!"

*An accurate one.* I turn the statement over in my head. I know what she means here. She's shown him a picture where it's obvious that I'm fat. Because you know the whole camera-adds-ten-pounds thing? That's true, but it can also subtract. The picture on my MySpace page makes me look a great deal slimmer than I actually am.

"You have to do this, Ryan," Kim says, squeezing my arm. "I really think it would be good for you."

"Where's the party?"

"More later," she says, motioning for me to keep it down. "I don't want anyone else to find out I'm setting you up with Dave Sheriden. They'll be pissed I didn't give them first dibs."

I look around the theater. There's no one even listening. "No one here knows us."

"You can never be too careful," she says, nudging me. "Now, watch the film."

I have a bad feeling about this Dave. If he's so hot, such

a great kisser, why doesn't she want him for herself? And if he's so hot that all these other girls are clamoring at his door, then why does he want to go on a blind date, anyway?

I ask her.

"He didn't," Kim admits. "But when I told him how sweet you are, and that you're a virgin, he got really excited. I think it made him want to go out with you more!"

Uh-oh. Warning bells go off in my head. "He probably wants to go out with me so badly because he's hoping to devirginize me!" I say, panicking. "He probably views me as some sort of a challenge."

"No, I don't think so." Her eyes don't leave the screen. "I think Dave's trying to turn over a new leaf. He told me how happy he was that I had a friend like you, a friend with strong values. He said it would be refreshing to spend the evening with someone who has a good moral character."

That sounds like a line if I've ever heard one. But I'm desperate for a change, desperate to try something new. And, besides, if it all goes to hell, I can blame it on Dr. Paige. She's the one who told me to find a date this week. And she told me to try something I swore I'd never do.

Going out with a "man ho" fits both of those categories.

"I'll do it," I say before I can talk myself out of it.

"Yay!" Kim clasps her hands together. "You're gonna love Dave. And don't be freaked out about all the girls he's hooked up with. I promise he's a sweet guy."

"Just the same, I'm taking my mom's car." I'm getting worried, so I throw in, "And I don't want to meet him at the party. I'll meet him at a public place, like Starbucks or something first."

"I'm sure that can be arranged," she teases.

After the movie we go back to my house and hang out for a little while. Kim doesn't stay too late. I've got a busy day tomorrow, and I want to make sure I'm well rested. My photography class starts at seven a.m. sharp, and then I'll be hooking up with Dave sometime in the evening.

I'm so nervous about everything that I wind up taking two Klonopin just to fall asleep.

WAKE UP FEELING LIKE I'M HUNGOVER. I CAN STILL FEEL the Klonopin coursing through my veins, even though it should have emptied out a few hours ago. I grab a quick cup of coffee and then my mom drives me over to Benjamin McGann's class.

We don't talk much in the car; we don't talk much ever, to be honest. Mostly small talk, about things like her work and my school. She wonders if I'm going to continue working as a photographer for the *Greenlee Gazette* now that I've landed a spot in this class.

"I'll probably have to give it up," I tell her, sipping from my travel mug.

"I thought you might get burned out," she says.

"It's not that. I just don't know if my schedule will allow me to do both. I already missed one assignment this morning. I was supposed to shoot the track-and-field meet at Boxton, but I had to get the photo assistant to do it."

"Hmm, that's a shame," Mom says, but I can tell she's not really paying attention. It's okay, though. I don't blame her. She and Mark got into a huge fight last night. I could hear him screaming at her, calling her a bitch and an assortment of other, more vile, names. She's trying to get him to do more around the house—mow the lawn, take out the garbage—but he doesn't want to. For her sake (and mine—and Mark's, if you actually stop to think about it), I hope she wins this battle.

Mom drops me off in front of the building, with a quick kiss good-bye. "Call my cell when you're finished and I'll swing back by and pick you up."

"Thanks!" I wave, heading up the stairs into the building.

We're meeting in the photo lab at a nearby college. The building is laid out poorly, and I have a little trouble finding where I'm going. Fortunately, I run into a guy who points me in the right direction.

Once there, I head inside and find a seat at one of the tables in the adjacent classroom.

I'm shocked to see Josh Lancaster standing near the door. Josh and I exchange a brief glance, the kind of "nod hello" you do when you barely know someone.

"Are you taking the Benjamin McGann workshop?" I ask.

"Yeah. You?"

I nod.

We sit down next to each other at one of the long tables, taking the last two empty seats.

There were ten slots for the class, and I've been wondering if any other Greenlee High students made the cut. I can't believe Josh is here. I remember hearing his SUV head out around six thirty this morning, but I didn't imagine he'd be coming here.

"I can't believe we're up this early." Josh yawns, and turns to face me.

"I know."

"I was out really late."

"Did you go watch Megan cheer at the game last night?" I ask. As soon as the words leave my mouth, I wish I could take them back. Megan is Josh's girlfriend, although I don't know either of them personally, so it sounds weird for me to know this much about their schedules.

"Yeah, it was a pretty good time." He yawns again. "What about you? Did you do anything fun?"

"I went to the movies with my friend Kimberlee."

"Kimberlee Johnston?" he asks.

"Uh-huh." I'm surprised. "You know her?"

"Yup." The way he says it, I briefly wonder if Josh is her fuck buddy or something.

"How?" I blurt out. Might as well get this out in the open.

"Her boyfriend, Taylor, was on the soccer team with me last year."

Oh, duh. I actually should have figured that out. "Yeah, I knew that," I say. "What I meant is, how do you know I've been hanging out with Kim?"

"I see her car around your house all the time," he says. "We live next door to each other, remember?"

Of course I remember. I just didn't think Josh did. He certainly never acts like it.

Before we can continue the conversation, the door swings

open and Benjamin McGann comes strolling in. He looks different from what I expected. I've seen so much of his work, but I don't think I've ever seen *him*. I expected him to be taller, more exotic looking. Maybe with a shaved head, like that photographer Niles Barker from *America's Next Top Model*. Ben is short—five four at most—and he's got dark black hair with specs of gray. His face is covered with scruff. He's wearing khaki pants and a big green sweater, even though it's ninety-eight degrees outside.

"I am Benjamin McGann," he says. "You will not call me Benjamin. You will not call me Ben."

"Mr. McGann—," someone begins.

"You will not call me Mr. McGann. I'm thirty-five. Don't make me feel fifty."

I stifle a laugh. Thirty-five might as well be fifty, as far as I'm concerned.

"Call me Benji."

"Like the dog," Josh whispers, and I bite my lip.

"I like perfection," Benji says, pacing the room. "I will not accept your photographs until they are perfect. In the beginning, it may take you two hundred frames to find a good shot, a half box of contact paper to get a good print." He stops pacing. "To get what *I* consider a good shot, a good print," he clarifies. "You will do it over and over *and over* again until your work is perfection."

Everyone's looking a little nervous. "Relax," he says. "You'll get the hang of it quicker than you think. I've seen all of your work. You all have considerable potential, or I wouldn't have accepted you in the course. It'll just take a little time before you get in sync with what I want." He claps his hands together. "Now! Did everyone bring their two rolls of film?"

We nod, producing them.

"Great! We're going to start right away. No sense teaching until I have something to critique. Go ahead and start processing your film. Once you're done with that, come find me in the darkroom. The rolling room is infinitesimal, so no more than two people in there at a time." Since Josh and I are sitting closest to him, he motions for us to go first. "I assume you know how this all works?" He doesn't wait for us to answer. "If not, don't bother wasting your time with this class. Go back to the beginner's level."

"I've printed before," I say.

"Me too," Josh chimes in.

We scurry nervously around the room. Everyone's watching us, twiddling their thumbs. There's really nothing anyone can do until they've processed their film. Processing black-and-white film is tedious work. You take your film into a special rolling room. If you've ever seen a darkroom in person or on TV, then you know it's not completely pitch-black. It's lit with low-grade red bulbs so you can see what you're doing.

The rolling room is not like that. It is completely, and totally, devoid of light. You have to go past several opaque black curtains and down a series of curved hallways with their walls painted black to get there. And trust me, if you think you've ever experience pitch-black before, you're wrong. You cannot see your hands in front of you. You cannot see the floor, the ceiling, shadows.

You start by cracking the shell of your film roll with a bottle opener. Then you unspool the film. You roll it, very carefully, around a spool that is then placed inside a light-safe canister. Then you take the canister back into the main brightly lit room and mix the chemicals together to process your film.

Josh and I make our way into the rolling room, our hands groping against the walls, emerging into solid black.

"There's a counter over here," he says. But I'm disoriented and I can't tell where he's coming from.

"Over here," he says again.

"I can't find it."

"Hold on, I'm—" We slam into each other. Hard.

"There you are," I joke, trying to cover the awkwardness of the situation. I'm glad he can't see anything. I'm blushing profusely. "Did you drop your film?" If you drop your film in the rolling room, you're screwed. It's absolutely impossible to find anything in there.

"No. You?"

"I'm good."

"Okay, here it is." Josh takes my hand in his and leads me to the counter.

"Thanks." I spread my supplies out. I can hear him clanking around beside me.

"So . . . what do you think of McGann? Excuse me . . . *Benji*."

"He seems cool."

"He seems . . . weird."

I laugh. "Yeah. That, too."

Our arms brush against each other, and we both flinch. "Sorry. God, this is awkward," Josh says. "Talk about close quarters."

"No lie."

"I can't wait to see your shots. I bet they're great."

"Thanks! I can't wait to see your stuff. Your yearbook work is always really good."

"Oh, you can't be too creative there. I only shoot those 'cause I have to," Josh says. "You know how it is. What kind of stuff do you shoot in your spare time?"

"People," I blurt out. "I almost exclusively photograph people."

"Like who?"

I crack open my first roll of film and begin pulling it free from the casing. "Friends, acquaintances. I sometimes shoot street scenes, but mostly I like photographing people I'm close to. I like getting shots of them that are kind of unexpected." I'm getting excited talking about this. Few things make me zone out like photography. It's amazing how easily all my worries have drifted out of my mind. Like my impending date with Doom (or Dave, as his name may be). And my horrible, nonexistent relationship with Noah. It's good to forget about that stuff for a while.

"Cool." Josh's arm brushes mine again. "So who's on these rolls? Anyone I know? Chelsea Ramsay? Kimberlee Johnston? Mark? Your mom?" he guesses. It's weird hearing him say their names. I always forget how well Josh used to know me, my family. Considering how little we've talked over the past seven years—the fat years—it's hard to even remember that he lives next door.

"No—"

"Oh, wait! Let me guess. Noah Fairbanks? That would be pretty cool."

And he's back.

"Actually, I didn't shoot people on these rolls." I grab the spool and begin winding my film around it.

"You didn't?" Josh sounds perplexed.

"I was trying to do something different, so I took a bunch of slice-of-life shots—you know, the kind of Americana thing Benjamin McGann does."

"Hmm . . . ," Josh says. "I don't think we're supposed to copy Benji's style. I think he wants to see what you do on your own."

I bristle at his criticism. "I don't know. I just felt like my work might not have been right for this class."

"Might as well take a chance," Josh says.

"Yeah, but the stuff I normally shoot is kind of . . . personal."

"So what? You've got to reveal something of yourself if you want it to be good. Just as long as you don't reveal your naked body." He laughs.

Is that a shot at my weight? I can't tell. The old Josh would never be mean to me that way. But I don't know him anymore.

"But my point is, you can't hold back or your work will suck."

"I just . . . I didn't think Benji would want to look at a bunch of photos of my friends and family. That's what I sent in to get accepted to this class." I crack open my second roll of film and begin rolling it around the spool. "I wanted to show him I have range."

"Then maybe it was the right move."

We finish rolling our film, then pack it into the light-safe canisters.

"Hey, you realize this is the longest conversation we've had in, I don't know, eight years?"

I can't believe he just said that. "Yeah, I realize. But I didn't think you did." I chew on my lip for a minute. Then I remember Dr. Paige's advice. Stop being passive. When you see an opportunity, take it. My mom's paying good money for my therapy. Might as well put it to use. "I didn't think you liked me very much."

"You thought I didn't like you?" He's incredulous. "That's not true at all! Why in the world would you think that?" Josh laughs.

"Because we used to be good friends. We never talk anymore." I've been waiting to say this to Josh for a long, long time now. I never thought I'd have the nerve. But it's easier to talk in here, in the vacuous black. I don't have to worry about all of my flaws. He can't see my fat thighs or my double chin or the splotchy way my face blushes when I'm anxious.

"We grew up, Ryan," he says. "People change. It's not that I didn't like you, but you and I have a different set of friends, we're into different stuff."

"Yes, our interests are totally different. I like photography and you like . . . photography."

"But it's not like our paths crossed because of it before."

"Josh! We're in the same history class. You live next door to me, for God's sake."

Josh chuckles. "I see what you mean. But you gotta understand—it's not like I've been avoiding you for the past few years. You haven't talked to me, either."

I had never considered this before. If a friendship falls away, I always assume it's because the other person doesn't want to be around me anymore. I always assume I like people a lot more than they like me.

"You're sort of . . . you know . . . popular. And I'm sort of not."

"Oh, please!" Josh is laughing hard now. "You're the one who cavorts with millionaire rock stars."

And, once again, Noah Fairbanks has wormed his way in. I swear to God, I will be known as the fat girl who dated Noah Fairbanks for the rest of my life.

"I'm just some guy on the soccer team."

"How could I forget?" I tease him. "You've got that big-ass bumper sticker on the back of your SUV."

"Ah, yes. 'Soccer players do it in eleven different positions,'" he recites.

"Cocky much?"

"Always, Ryan. Always." He laughs. "False confidence is a great thing. Much better than real insecurity."

That's a weird thing for him to say. "Do you think—"

"Come on, let's go back out," he says. "We're holding up the group. You're finished, right? I haven't heard you moving around for a few minutes."

"Yeah, I'm finished." But I don't want to leave. This is nice. Reassuring, somehow.

Josh takes my hand and leads me back through the maze. My palm is sweaty—really, grossly sweaty. It wasn't this way before. I'm nervous now. We emerge back into the light, which is blinding.

We've been gone awhile, and I halfway expect people to crack jokes about us making out. In the last photography class I took—the one taught by the heinous Kirby—everyone used to joke about people kissing and having sex in the rolling room. Then again, I think Kirby was the one who started that. Things in Benji's class are very different. No one says a word. The next twosome merely gets up and files into the dark.

Since we're ahead of the group, Josh and I go over to the sink and start pulling out the various chemicals needed to turn the unprocessed film into negatives. I pour the requisite amount of developer into the canister and start shaking it up so it will cover all of the film. I continue on, pouring out the developer and moving on to the next chemical. It's not a complicated process, but Josh and I don't talk at all while we work.

I wonder if this is the way it's going to be? One great conversation, and then we don't talk again for five years.

The rest of the class goes by in a blur. Benji is pretty hands-off at the moment. He wants us to make two prints and leave them tacked up on the board out front. He'll spend the week critiquing them and give us his opinion next class. We also have to leave our negatives and contact sheets so he can get the full scope of what we're working on.

I time it so I leave at the same moment as Josh. I'm sort of wondering if he'll offer to give me a ride home so I don't have to call my mom. We live next door; it would only make sense.

But he doesn't wait around for me. Just hustles off toward the parking lot and leaves without saying good-bye.

# *Freudian Slips*

## DR. PAIGE NORRIS, PhD, MD

PATIENT: *Ryan Burke*

PERSONAL GOALS FOR THE WEEK

1. *Do not tell a single lie.*
   *Live honestly. Fully.*

# Chapter Five

MY MOTHER DOES NOT WANT ME GOING ON THIS date.

"I have no idea who this Dave person is," she says, sounding angry, "and I can't believe you'd plan something like this without, *at the very least*, inviting him over first so I can meet him."

"Mom, he's a good friend of Kimberlee's."

"That's not making me feel more comfortable. I've seen what some of Kimberlee's friends are like."

This is my own fault. I was afraid my mom would have a problem with this date, so I waited until the last possible minute to tell her.

"Dave's a really nice guy," I say, hoping my ears aren't turning pink. That always happens when I lie.

"Then why isn't he stopping by the house first so I can meet him?"

"He's getting off work late," I ad-lib, "so I'm meeting him there."

"Well, unless he comes over here first, then you can't go."

"Mom!" I wail.

"I'm serious about this, Ryan. No ifs, ands, or butts about it. If he won't come over here, then you can't go out."

"Fine. It shouldn't be a problem." And I know this is true. When I spoke to Dave on the phone earlier he seemed annoyed that I wanted to meet him at Starbucks.

"I don't get off work until seven o'clock and the party starts at five thirty," he said. "We're already going to be really late as it is, and you're pushing things back even more. It would be so much easier if I could just pick you up and we could go straight there."

I knew he was full of shit. What kind of party starts at five thirty on a Saturday night? Most things don't get going until nine or ten. Eight at the absolute earliest. Dave was obviously inventing a story so he could get me alone in the car. Which is kind of scary, if you think about it. But I couldn't tell Mom this.

"I'll let him know right away."

I begrudgingly text Dave that there's been a change of plans and give him directions to our house. "He's coming to pick me up," I say, through gritted teeth. "Are you happy now?"

"Yes, very."

This is exactly why parents shouldn't interfere. Before, my plan was airtight safe, totally secure. I would never be alone in the car with Dave and I'd have my own ride home in case things got sketchy. And I was meeting him for coffee first so I could size him up. If I'd spied anything suspicious going on at Starbucks, I could have cut and run. Now, I'll be stuck with Dave all night, no matter what. *Swell.*

Plus, now my mother is going to meet him at the exact same time that I do. Considering I've never even seen a picture of Dave before, this could be disastrous. What if he's a total freak, with a million piercings or tattoos? What if he's three hundred pounds of solid muscle? What if he drives a motorcycle, wears a leather jacket? What if he shows up reeking of beer? Or, worse yet, what if he gets completely drunk at the party and then I'm forced to bum a ride with someone else?

See, Mom really should have trusted me in the first place. Things would have been so much simpler.

Kimberlee comes over around five thirty to help me get ready. I've laid out a bunch of outfits on my bed—tops and pants from Lane Bryant, Torrid, Old Navy. She vetoes everything.

"Don't you have any sexy little dresses or short skirts you can wear?"

"No," I say, feeling irritated, "these are the best things I own."

"Maybe we should go shopping. Do you think we have time?"

"No," I say firmly. "We do not."

"Hmm." Kim surveys the pile again and finally selects a pair of loose black pants and a baggy red shirt. "Put these on."

I do, and she makes a face.

"Look, I know what you're trying to do here, Ryan," Kimberlee says. "I'm not stupid."

"What do you mean, you know what I'm trying to do?" I figure she's going to say that I'm dressing conservatively because I'm afraid of Big Bad Dave and his fifty zillion sexual partners.

"You do this because you're not happy with your body."

"Do what?" I blush. I don't like it when anyone talks about my body. Period.

"Buy clothes that don't fit."

I'm taken aback. I was expecting her to make a comment

113

about sex. "What do you mean? These clothes fit." I would never dream of buying something too small.

"They're loose as hell," she says.

"That's because I don't want to show off my fat rolls," I say. Might as well be honest.

"I know, and I think that's dumb."

"W-what?" I stutter. "You think I should show off my fat rolls?"

"Yeah, I do. When you wear clothes that are about three sizes too big, you look like you have no shape. So what if it hugs your fat? You still end up looking smaller in the end. And"—Kim says, reaching out and patting my hand—"guys don't care so much if you've got a little bit of extra padding."

Like *she* would know!

"They still want to see something that's tight on your boobs. And if it shows a roll of fat on your stomach, so be it!" She grins. "If your tits are on parade, they're not going to be looking down there, trust me."

I don't, not really, but I agreed to take her advice, at least for tonight. Dave is her friend, after all. Kim takes my red Old Navy shirt—which at a size twenty *is* pretty loose—and safety pins it in the back so it hugs tightly across my chest. She then takes off the black sash she's wearing and ties it around me, making a bow in the back to cover the safety pin. I have to admit, it does look a ton better this way.

Kim flat-irons my hair, puts on my makeup, and then leaves. "Call me when you get home. I don't care how late it is."

"I will," I promise.

"Have a good time." She winks at me.

"I hope I do."

"Oh, you definitely will," Kim says, kissing me on the cheek.

We say good-bye, and I go downstairs to wait.

DAVE ARRIVES TWENTY MINUTES EARLY. MY mother gets to the door before I do and she lets him inside. I hurry over. I'm dying to catch a glimpse of him, dying to see what Kimberlee's friend is all about.

When I see him, I'm shocked. He's tall, beanpole thin, and nerdy. Not at all the kind of guy I'd picture hitting on tons of girls. He looks like a pre-record-company makeover Noah Fairbanks.

"It's nice to meet you, Mrs. Ryan," he says, and I nearly die. He doesn't even know my name!"

"Um, it's Burke. *Ms.* Burke. But you can call me Mallory."

"Okay, Mallory," he says. "I'm David."

"Hi," I call out, coming over. "I'm Ryan."

My mother gives me a look, as if to say, *You didn't tell me this was a blind date!*

Dave and I shake hands. I'm trying to gauge his reaction. Now that he's seen me, is he happy? Disappointed? His face doesn't give anything away.

"Where are you two going tonight?" my mom asks.

"Church," he says. I grimace. He's laying it on a little thick. My God, he could have said we were going to a movie or something believable.

"Church?" Mom seems taken aback. My family's not very religious, and, other than Andrew, I've never shown much interest in Christian boys. If only she knew the truth about Dave. "Well, that's nice. Are they having a Saturday service?" she asks. Uh-oh. She's suspicious.

"No, ma'am." Dave grins. "They're having a fall carnival-slash-party," he says. "It's for the youth group. Even though I'm nineteen, I've volunteered to go along and help out. I thought Ryan and I could lead some of the games and activities."

Now this is getting ridiculous. My mother is never going to buy this crap! But, amazingly, she does. "Well, have a nice time, then," she says. "Call if you're going to be late."

We walk outside and climb into his Saturn.

"Okay, Dave, where are we really going?" I ask, once he's backed out of the driveway. I've been so keyed up about this date, but now that it's actually happening, I'm pretty excited. I can't wait to see where he's taking me.

"Holloway Baptist Church."

Something in his tone tells me he's not joking. "Are you serious?"

"Yes."

"We're going to a church carnival?"

"Uh-huh." He flips on the radio and turns it to the easy-listening station. An old Barry Manilow song begins to play.

"I didn't know that was your sort of thing."

"It is." Dave begins whistling along to the tune.

"But Kimberlee told me—"

At the mention of Kim's name, his face clouds over. "Kimberlee Johnston does not know me anymore," he says. "She doesn't know who I am now."

"Uh, okay. And who are you?" I ask.

"I'm a born-again," he says.

"Christian?"

"Virgin."

Born-again virgin? Does such a thing even exist? I mean,

once you lose the big V, you can't ever get it back. Not really.

"But I am something of a born-again Christian, now that you mention it," he adds.

"I thought you'd slept with more than fifty people," I blurt out. This is a horrible thing to say, but I can't help myself.

"I do not discuss my past," Dave says firmly. "I am only concerned with the future."

I'm starting to wonder if Kimberlee set me up as some kind of cruel joke. Why tell me he's a male slut if he's actually not?

"I joined Holloway Baptist Church last spring," Dave explains. "It turned my entire life around. A few months later, I became a member of TW-squared—Teens Who Wait."

I'm at a loss for words. An abstinence club?

"Teens Who Wait," I muse. "That's nice."

"It's more than *nice*. Joining TW-squared was the best decision I ever made. Before TW-squared, I was swimming in a wasteland of immorality. Now I make it my personal goal to instill good, proper values in all of the people I meet. You'll find out more about that as the night goes on."

I stifle a giggle. This is ludicrous. He's staring at me with this gravely serious look in his eyes, as though I'm some big sinner and he's here to save me. Yet, up until a few months ago, the guy was sleeping with anything that moved. It seems a little hypocritical.

"There isn't a day that goes by that I don't regret my past sexual escapades," he continues, as if reading my mind. "I wish I'd never done those things, had those partners. That's why I called Kimberlee Johnston yesterday. That's a girl who needs help if there ever was one. I was planning to bring her to the carnival, to surprise her with my newfound spirituality. But then she told me she was busy." He smiles. "But I'm so glad you were free. When she told me you were a virgin, I couldn't have been more thrilled. That you've managed to hang on to your womanhood is a wonderful thing. I can't wait to get you involved with Holloway and TW-squared. You're going to fit right in."

So this was never a date to begin with; it was a recruitment. "Well, uh . . ." I'm at a loss for words.

Dave, on the other hand, seems to have plenty to say. "At TW-squared we promote a healthy understanding of human sexuality, with an emphasis on abstinence-based education and practices." It sounds like he's reading from a brochure. "Not only is sex before marriage morally and socially wrong, but it leads to low self-esteem, poor decision making, and— even death!"

"Death?" I ask, confused.

"AIDS," he says, shaking his head in horror.

"Oh, right."

"Sex before marriage has no meaning," Dave says. "Trust me, I know." He stops the car in front of an enormous church. "We're here," he says, climbing out of the driver's seat.

I'm not sure what to do. Do I follow him inside and go to the carnival, or do I call my mom and beg her to come pick me up?

I decide to give it a shot. It's not that I'm antireligion or anything. But big church functions have never been my thing.

And I don't want to join an abstinence club. I don't want to wear a bracelet on my arm that says EVERYTHING GOOD IS WORTH WAITING FOR. I don't want to take a vow of celibacy that might last . . . God knows how long. I'm almost eighteen now. It could be another decade or so before I get married. Not to sound like a horndog, but that's a long, long time.

We walk into a brightly lit church gym. My cell phone starts going off as I get inside. I expect it to be Kimberlee, calling to find out how the date is going. But it's not. It's a text message, from Chelsea.

*Won't b back at Greenlee 4 a while. Staying 4 the 1st*

*semester of school. B back in December b4 the start of spring*
*term. Sorry 2 tell u like this but I wanted 2 let u know rite away.*

I stare at the message, stunned. But I don't have much time
to process it. Dave is grabbing my hand, leading me over to
the far wall.

"I've signed us up to lead Pin the Tail on the Biblical
Donkey."

"What?"

"The rules are simple," he says as we hurry over. "We ask
the children a question from the Bible and then whoever gets
it right wins a chance to pin the tail on Joseph's donkey. If
they manage to connect, then they get a prize. The prizes are
crosses, Bible bookmarks, etc."

"That sounds lovely," I say. I'm still thinking about
Chelsea's message, trying to take it all in.

"Hey, Dave—" I'm about to ask where the bathrooms
are—I need to splash some cold water on my face—but he
cuts me off.

"Please," he says. "I don't like being called that anymore.
I go by David now."

"Of course," I say, following him over to Joseph's donkey.
I ready myself for a long night.

It's ironic. I'm in a church, yet I'm on the date from hell.

\* \* \*

'M GOING TO CALL NOAH. I MADE THE DECISION SOME-
where between Chelsea's "I'm not coming home" text
message and Pin the Tail on the Biblical Donkey.

I realized that I've been avoiding Noah because I'm afraid.
What does it really matter if I crash and burn? Tonight has
been so disastrous, so f'd up, that I might as well go for
broke.

And going for broke means calling Noah and telling him
how much he means to me, telling him how much I still care
about him. It's not that I want to get back together with him;
I know that will never happen. Noah's dating some girl from
*Laguna Beach* (at least according to Perez Hilton's blog). But
Noah was an important part of my life. He treated me so
well, accepted me, weight and all. And in return, I put him
down, I tried to change him, to make him over into someone
cooler. It embarrassed me that he didn't care what people
thought of him. I was a horrible girlfriend at times, and I wish
I could take that back.

There are other, more important things I need to say.

I loved him once. And he needs to know that.

My excuse—my lead-in to the conversation—will be
that I want to tell him about the Benjamin McGann class.

Noah was always so supportive of my photography; I know he'll be thrilled for me. Besides, everyone's right. There's no reason why Noah and I shouldn't talk more often. Nothing's stopping us.

I contemplate calling Kimberlee first. I did promise to call as soon as I got back from my date with Dave—excuse me, DAVID—and give her the full scoop. But I don't feel like going into that now.

I do try Chelsea's cell phone, but—surprise, surprise!—she doesn't pick up. I have probably called her ten times in the past week, sent her a dozen or more e-mails. No response, until that stupid text message tonight. At first I was worried. But when I noticed that she's been logging on to MySpace every day, posting comments on other people's pages, I got angry. If she's too busy to talk, that's one thing. But she's obviously got enough time to surf MySpace. Why doesn't she have time to send me a quick, one-sentence e-mail to tell me she's okay? To tell me the reason why she's not coming back? To tell me what the hell is going on in her life? Why she no longer seems to want to be friends . . .

I push the thought out of my head. I'm not going to stress out about Chelsea right now, not going to let the fact that she's avoiding me—and that she used a text message to tell me that she's not coming home this semester—bring me down. I've had a crappy enough day. I need to focus on happy things.

Like Noah Fairbanks.

I take a few deep breaths. My hands are shaking.

I'm just going to do it. I look through my cell phone. I have him listed under the name Kelly. It's a code. I couldn't list him under his real name. I know this sounds paranoid, but I have my reasons. When Noah first got famous last Christmas, I was deluged with requests for info. Suddenly, everyone in school wanted to be my best friend because they thought I could link them up to him. One girl, a bitchy senior named Abby Brewer, hacked into my AOL account and tried to get Noah's e-mail address. I was stupid enough to make the password something really obvious—Ryan16: my first name, plus my age at the time—so I guess I deserved it. Abby struck out. I've never stored anything in my AOL address book, and I delete the contents of my inbox daily. As soon as I found out what happened (I overheard two of Abby's friends talking about it in the chem lab), I changed my password. Still, the close call has left me scared.

Am I really going to go through with this? What will I say? I rehearse the conversation in my mind, remembering what I'd talked about earlier with Kimberlee. I'll ask him how the album's going, when the new single will be out, if he wants me to throw him a release party here in Atlanta.

We'll make small talk, and somewhere between "How's the weather in L.A.?" and "Everyone at school really misses you," the ice will be broken and it will be just like old times. Just like when we were in love.

Before I can talk myself out of it, I dial his number.

I halfway expect him not to answer. It's been more than two months since we last spoke, and Noah changes his number frequently.

But he picks up on the fourth ring. "Ryan," he says, not bothering with hello.

My heart skips a beat. He must have seen my number pop up on the caller ID and instantly recognized that it was me! All those years of dialing my digits must have emblazoned them into his brain. "I didn't know you had my number memorized."

"I don't." He sounds distant, tired. "You're programmed into my phone. Your name popped up on my screen."

"I'm so glad you answered," I gush. Wow, way to sound insecure!

"I almost didn't. I was about to go into a party. But I figured I've got three minutes to chat."

"Three minutes," I tease. "Is that all I'm worth? Can't I at least get the requisite five?"

He doesn't play along with the joke. "What's up?"

This is off to a less-than-stellar start. "I just . . . I haven't talked to you in a really long time, Noah."

"Sure."

"And I wondered how you were."

"I'm good. Busy." He coughs. "The song will be out in a few weeks. . . . I just saw the final cut for the video."

"What's it called?"

"Can't you look this up on Google?" he snaps.

"Oh, um, yeah. I suppose."

"Because I kind of don't have time to go into all of this now. There's people waiting. I have stuff to do."

Suddenly I feel like I'm going to cry. He's like a stranger to me, and a jerk! How is this the guy I once felt so comfortable around? We weren't great as lovers (we weren't technically ever lovers), but we were awesome as friends. We still kept in touch after we broke up. I went around his house to watch movies every now and then. We even drove go-karts together.

I can't really remember how we lost touch completely. When Noah moved to New York for college, our conversations got less frequent. A few weeks passed and I didn't hear anything from him. Then six months. Suddenly, one day, he called out of the blue. It was the afternoon he'd gotten the offer from BMG. I didn't even realize he was actively pursuing a music career. I knew it was important to him. I knew he was a songwriter and a performer, of course. But I never thought he'd cross that line, take that step. I never thought he'd get out there and perform at music showcases, cut a demo, hire a manager.

It all seemed so bold, so unlike the Noah Fairbanks I used to know. That Noah had panic attacks at the thought of performing in the school talent show. That Noah was happier in his parents' basement, with his Xbox, his *Lord of the Rings* DVDs.

I'll never forget when he called to tell me the news. I remember the tone of his voice—shocked, scared, ecstatic. He was feeling so many emotions, I'm sure, and in typical Noah fashion, he didn't know how to express any of them.

We were alike in that way. His music always has been the place he poured everything out. With me, it's my photography. Neither of us has ever been good at saying things outright. Maybe that was why our relationship stalled. Maybe that was why we grew apart.

The record deal was like the final nail in the coffin. Any closeness we still shared evaporated soon afterward. It shouldn't have been that way, but it was. I mostly blame myself. I didn't want to seem overeager. I didn't want to chase after him, come across like a phony friend using him for his stardom. So I didn't call, and I didn't write often.

After Noah got the recording contract, nothing happened for a while. News spread pretty fast around Greenlee. At the time everyone was a critic. And a lot of them seemed to be rooting for his failure. *He's probably making it up. Exaggerating, at the very least. I bet the album never comes out. And even if it does, do you know how many people get major-label releases and crash and burn? It's not like he's going to be a twenty-first-century Elvis Presley or something. We'll never hear him on the radio, never see him on MTV. And when the album tanks, he'll have to pay BMG back all the money they've put into him. He'll probably owe them, like, $500,000. Wow, I wouldn't want to be in his predicament. Nineteen years old and in debt for half a million dollars. I hope his parents haven't spent their life savings, 'cause they'll be bailing him out. I can't imagine what it's going to be like to fail on that kind of level, in such a public—and costly—way.*

I listened to that talk for a year. An entire year of feeling sick to my stomach, of dreading Noah's release. I worried that the naysayers were right. I was terrified for him. Even though he was two years older, and a guy, I'd always felt protective of him. He had meant so much to me. I wondered if he knew that? I wanted to tell him, but I couldn't make myself say the words. He's probably so jaded that they wouldn't mean much.

Because once his first single came out—once it charted and the video went into heavy rotation on MTV and he started making appearances on *TRL*—everything exploded. His worst enemies were now his best friends.

And I was nobody.

But, still, I'd like to believe that I meant something in his life.

"Look, Ryan, I'm sorry. I'm not in a great mood. You've caught me at a bad time. I haven't slept in two days. I've been running around so much."

"I'm sorry."

"Don't be." His voice softens. "I do want to talk to you. Actually, I kind of *need* to talk to you."

"Really?" My pulse quickens. I can't figure out what this means.

"It's about my new single, 'Girl on Ice,' he says, laughing.

"That's the title. See, you don't have to Google it after all. I'm sorry I was being an ass a minute ago. I should have just told you when you asked."

"That's okay." I'm thoroughly confused.

"See, I'm really excited about my new song, but I want you to be excited too. Are you excited about it?"

I'm starting to think he's high. Which would be weird, since Noah's very antidrugs. He even freaked out when I let it slip a few months ago that I'd started taking Zoloft and Klonopin. Noah has suffered from panic attacks for most of his life, yet he's never used medication. He thought it was sad that I caved in the second a doctor offered them to me.

"Yes! I'm very excited!"

"It's a little bit inspired by you," Noah says. "Just a little, little bit. So don't sue me, okay? Not that you'd win against my army of lawyers." He laughs again.

I'm speechless. Completely, totally speechless. A full minute passes before I know what to say. "Excuse me . . . did I just hear that right? Did you just tell me that your new song was inspired by me?" My voice is barely above a whisper.

"A little, little, little bit. But also some other people too."

I don't care who these "other people" are. I'm going to pretend it's all about me. "I'm, uh, I'm so flattered, I don't know what to say."

"I'll have my publicist overnight you a copy of the single," he promises. "That way, you can hear it early and tell me what you think."

"I. Would. Love. That." I'm measuring my words carefully. I'm in a major daze.

"You still at the same address?"

"Yes."

He doesn't respond.

"Noah?"

Still nothing.

"Noah? NOAH!"

I hear him scuffling around. "Sorry, I dropped my phone on the pavement. What did you say?"

"I said I still live at the same address."

"Excellent. I think I remember it. If not, I'll have Sheila call you to get the info."

"Is Sheila your publicist?"

"Yes." He hiccups. "I'm a little drunk right now, if you can't tell."

"No, I can't," I lie. I take a deep breath. Here's my chance, my opportunity to tell him how I feel. He's given me the perfect opening, telling me about the song.

"Okay, Ryan, I've gotta go. Nice talking to you. Don't be such a stranger, darlin'."

Darlin'? It's funny hearing him talk like that. Since getting famous Noah has affected this weird Southern accent. Which is strange, since he never sounded like that when he lived here. I don't see how moving from Georgia to New York could make a person more countrified, but whatever. I figure it's all a part of his carefully crafted image.

He hangs up the phone before I have the chance to say good-bye, but I'm not offended. I can't stop thinking about what's just happened.

Holy mother of God (see, David is rubbing off on me after all).

Noah Fairbanks has written a song about me!

# *Freudian Slips*

## DR. PAIGE NORRIS, PhD, MD

PATIENT: *Ryan Burke*

PERSONAL GOALS FOR THE WEEK

1. *Try to address some of your family issues—particularly the ones involving your brother— head-on.*

# Chapter Six

I TELL EVERYONE I KNOW ABOUT THE SONG. THIS MAY not be the wisest idea, considering I haven't heard it yet. But I can't help myself. I'm beyond excited, and I'm unable to contain it.

Kimberlee and I spend an hour on the phone, talking about anything and everything. She's horrified by Dave's weird behavior.

"I'm so sorry. If I had any idea what a punk he'd turned into, I never would have introduced you," she apologizes.

"No worries," I say. "You were only trying to help."

The talk shifts to Noah and the song. Neither of us can figure out what the title means.

"No offense, *chica*, but 'Girl on Ice' is kind of a stupid title."

"No way," I argue.

"It sounds like it should be about Michelle Kwan or Sarah Hughes or something."

I laugh. "Nope. It's about me."

Kim thinks it over. "Well . . . I guess you keep things on ice when you want to preserve them. That's another way to think of it."

"Maybe he wants to preserve our love?"

"I was talking more literally . . . like, literally, a girl on ice."

"Ew." I grimace. "Like the way serial killers keep a human body in the freezer?" I'm hating the title now too.

"I was thinking more like a heart for a transplant patient."

"That could be kind of romantic."

"Please don't look for hidden meaning in this," she says, sounding worried. "Please don't think Noah did this so he can get back with you."

"I don't think that."

"You sure?"

"Absolutely," I say. But I'm lying, and we both know it.

"When are you getting the CD?"

"I don't know," I say. "Soon, I hope. He told me he'd overnight me an advance copy, so hopefully I'll have it by Monday."

But I do not get the single on Monday.

Then a week passes and still nothing. I'm starting to wonder if Noah made the whole thing up. I try calling him again, but he doesn't answer. I write him on AOL, but he leaves the messages unread.

"I GOT AN INTERESTING CALL TODAY," MOM SAYS. IT'S Monday night, and we're seated around the dinner table— all of us. Me, Mark, and my grandfather. The only one missing is Grandma, who has a book club meeting tonight.

"Speaking of calls, did you ever contact Erica Kloos?" Grandpa pipes up.

Mark snickers, and I kick him under the table.

I take a deep breath. "No, and I'm not going to."

"Well, I think you should."

I try to remain calm. "I appreciate your advice, but I think I'm going to have to take a pass."

"Take a pass?" he repeats. "Just call her, Ryan," he says impatiently. "It'll do you a lot of good."

"I'm not interested but thanks," I say.

"You're not interested in losing weight?" he asks, and I feel stung. Do we really have to have this conversation?

"I'm not interested in talking to Erica Kloos."

"Leave her alone, Dad," Mom chimes in. "Ryan's perfectly capable of making her own decisions."

"She's being stubborn," he says.

"No, *you're* being stubborn," Mom tells him. "Just drop it."

He snorts. "That's the problem with this family. No discipline. These kids do something wrong, do something bad in their lives, and you do nothing to help them straighten it out."

There's an uncomfortable silence, and then Mom tries to change the subject. She usually does this when Grandpa starts to get on one of his big rampages.

"I mean, look at Mark," he says, unable to let it go.

I jerk to attention. *Look at Mark?* Well, there's a new one. No one ever gets on Mark's case. This I want to hear.

"Can we drop this, please?" Mom begs.

He doesn't. "I offered him that internship at my firm, and what does he do? He doesn't even bother to show up on his first day of work."

Whoa. This is news to me. I stare at Mark, whose head is bowed. Probably trying to hide his bloodshot eyes. Although, in all fairness, I have noticed his pot use has slacked off a bit lately. Instead of being high seven days a week, he seems to be saving it more for Friday and Saturday nights. I think it's due to his new schedule at Walgreens. He used to work really erratic hours—one day he'd be on mornings, the next evenings—so he never really got a proper weekend. But now that he's working eight to five, Monday through Friday, he seems happier. He's been going out more, seeing some of his old friends. Not being fucked up all the time. But this internship . . . what's this all about?

"I'm trying to get you a good job," Grandpa says, his tone angry. "A part-time data entry clerk pays a hell of a lot more than the six dollars an hour you make as a checker. And this could be a real career stepping-stone for you. If you like it, you could go on to get an associate's degree in accounting or, let's not get carried away here, maybe even a bachelor's!"

I've never seen him this worked up about Mark before, and it's fun to watch. Mostly because it's not about me. They argue about it for a few more minutes, and then Mom asks me to leave the table. "Do you mind eating in the other room?"

I pick up my plate of veggie casserole and traipse off to the den. *Damn!* I really wanted to stay and witness this. By the time I finish eating, their fight is over. With all the excitement, I've completely forgotten about Mom's "interesting call." Apparently, she did too.

She comes running into my room as I'm getting ready for bed later that night.

"Ryan!" she says. "I can't believe I forgot to tell you this. I was telling all the girls at my work about Noah's new song—they're all big fans, of course." Mom works as a paralegal at a large law firm downtown. There are lots of college interns running around who always beg Mom for the scoop on Noah. "Anyway, one of the girls is friends with Marilyn Roberts's cousin. You know, Marilyn, the local news anchor. Anyway, she told Marilyn about how you and Noah used to date, and how his new single was inspired by you. Anyway, Marilyn Roberts wants to interview you for a human interest piece!"

I bolt upright in bed. "What?!" I shriek. This is pretty major.

"Marilyn called me today when I was on my way home from work. She wants to come by Wednesday evening to do the interview. I told her that I'd have to check with you, of course, but that I thought it would be okay." Mom pauses.

"Yes! Absolutely! Oh, my God, this is going to be the coolest thing ever!"

"I know," Mom says, squeezing me on the shoulder. "I know."

T IS NOT THE COOLEST THING EVER.

As I sit in my living room Wednesday night decked out in a bright pink sweater and blue jeans (my original outfit was vetoed by the cameraman—apparently all black is not a good look for TV), I want to disappear into the floorboards.

The very first question out of Marilyn Roberts's mouth is, "Has Noah Fairbanks always liked bigger girls?"

I have no idea how to answer this. I turn about twenty shades of red, and beads of sweat start to form across my upper lip. "I don't know much about Noah's other girl-friends," I manage to say. "Just myself."

"And you're a big girl," Marilyn says. She's smiling at me the entire time, as though we're great friends and I should just relax and not pay attention to the dagger she's shoving in my back. "That's somewhat unusual, to have a sexy heartthrob like Noah Fairbanks date a big girl. Was he ever bothered by your weight? Did he comment on it much?"

"No," I yelp.

"Is he attracted to bigger women?"

"Didn't you already ask that?" I point out. "I told you I'm not sure."

"Tell us about the song Noah wrote for you. 'Girl on Ice.' What exactly does that mean?"

"I'm not sure exactly," I admit. I'm choosing my words carefully. I don't want to walk into a land mine.

"So you haven't heard the song?"

"No."

"And then how do you know it's about you?"

"Noah told me."

"So you guys keep in really close touch!" she says, her enthusiasm bubbling over.

The lights are so hot. I'm starting to sweat on my hairline now, too. "Not exactly."

"But you must have talked pretty recently, in order for you to have found out about the song."

"We talk off and on."

"And what are those conversations like? What kinds of things does he tell you about?"

"His career. His music. What he's been doing in New York or L.A."

"Mmm-hmm," she says. "Speaking of L.A., are there a lot of fat girls in that part of the country? Anyone Noah has mentioned . . ."

"IT WASN'T THAT BAD," MOM SAYS AS WE SIT AROUND the kitchen table after the interview is over.

"It was awful!" I wail. "The worst thing I've ever experienced in my life."

Mark walks into the kitchen to fix a glass of chocolate

milk. I wish he'd leave. I don't want to hear his smart-ass comments. But for once, he doesn't make any.

"Yeah, Ryan's right. That woman was a bitch," he says. Then he comes over and gives me a quick hug. "But don't let her get to you. The story'll air next week and then everybody will forget about it. You'll see."

I hope he's right. But deep down, I'm worried.

ENJAMIN MCGANN HATES ME.

Saturday morning, he pulls out the photo I took of an old-fashioned Southern porch and holds it up in front of the room.

"This is an example of exactly what *not* to do," he announces.

I feel my face scorching with embarrassment.

"Who took this picture?"

I don't want to claim ownership, but I have to. All he has do is look at the negatives—which are in a folder with my name on it—and he'll know exactly who did it.

I slowly raise my hand. "That's mine."

"What's your name?"

"Ryan Burke," I say meekly.

"Well, Ryan Burke, you've certainly failed to impress me

on your first attempt." He looks me directly in the eyes. "I sincerely hope this isn't your best work."

My mouth opens, then closes, then opens again. I probably look like a blowfish, puffing away. But I can't think of how to respond. If I say it's not my best work, he'll scold me for turning in something subpar. But if I say it's the best I can do, he might kick me out of the class. "I think I can do better," I finally say.

"I hope so," he says, "for both our sakes. Because this is an absolute waste of film."

I've never been publicly criticized like this in my life. I feel myself buckling under the weight of his words.

"Now, who wants to critique this work?" he asks, tacking my print onto the board. "Who wants to point out all the things—and there are many—that are wrong with it?"

I expect no one to volunteer, out of courtesy, but every hand in the room goes up, Josh's included. Wow. Way to throw me under the bus. I figured at the very least he would be loyal to me. But then, why should he be? We're not friends, as he keeps reminding me. Oh, he's friendly enough. Cordial, you might call it. He waves when we pass each other in the halls, says hi in history class. But he never talks to me at school, never calls or drops by my house to see what I'm doing, despite the fact that we live next door.

Benji selects a short redhead named Gwen Landry. She goes up to the board and begins raking me over the coals, pointing out how awful my work is. Although she does pause to give credit to my technical skills. The focus, light, framing. That's all fine. I've even done a fair job of printing from the negative.

"But, stylistically, this is terrible," she concludes.

"Go on."

"It's really not intriguing enough."

"Be more specific."

"Something's missing."

"Something what?"

Gwen struggles for an answer. "I can't quite put my finger on it."

Benji sighs. "In the future, Gwen, please do not volunteer to critique a print if you don't have something intelligent to say."

She blushes, and I'm glad that, for a moment at least, someone else is taking the heat.

But soon enough we're back to me.

"Who else would like to take a stab at this?"

Josh's hand flies up and, this time, Benji selects him.

"The problem is, the photograph doesn't feel authentic," Josh begins. "It's like the artist tried to copy an existing style rather than develop a style of her own." Benji nods, so he continues. "The whole experience is artificial. It feels like a rip-off, a bad imitation of something I've seen a thousand times before."

"Exactly!" Benji claps his hands together. "You've hit it on the head."

I want to hit *him* on the head. Him being Josh.

He gives me an apologetic half smile. "Traitor," I mutter under my breath, and he looks genuinely hurt. But I can't help it. The only reason he knew to say that was because of what I told him when we were in the rolling room.

After Benji finishes slamming my photos, he shifts focus. "Now that we've discussed the worst photos of the class, let's do the best." I know this is mean, but I'm secretly glad that Josh doesn't win this honor. I'm a little pissed off at him right now, even though I know that's not fair. He was just trying to impress Benji, same as everyone else.

The rest of the class is tedious. I don't like being here, feeling like the class failure. And I'm worried. Since Benji hated my other prints so much, I don't know what he's going to think of my new stuff. I've produced two more rolls of the same, "artificial" work, and I know he's going to hate it.

I'm getting ready to call my mom, when Josh stops me. "I'll take you home," he says, smiling. "We're practically going to the same place."

The drive home is tense, at first. I stare straight ahead while Josh makes small talk about class. Suddenly, he says, "I didn't mean to hurt your feelings. I'm sorry."

I sigh. "It's okay. It's not your fault. It just sucks being called out like that. And"—I hesitate, unsure of how to say this—"part of what upsets me is that I know you're right. I know my photographs weren't very good, and I don't know how to fix that."

"Take good shots next time."

"Yeah, but what if I can't? What if I'm not cut out for this?"

"You are," Josh assures me. "I've seen your other stuff. It's excellent."

"Thank you." I blush.

"You just have to go back to doing what you do best— portraits, people, whatever. Don't try to be something you're not."

I agree. "You're right. The only sucky thing is, I've just

handed in two more awful rolls of prints. I didn't know how much Benji would hate my Americana stuff until today. So I shot more rolls of crap."

"Call him," Josh says firmly.

"Who? Benji?"

He nods. "Call him and tell him what you've done. Ask him if you can throw out what you've handed in today and start over. Tell him you'll work double time, shoot them this week and bring them to his office as soon as possible." He glances over at me. "I'm serious, Ryan. This course is a once-in-a-lifetime thing, and it's only twelve weeks long. You can't afford to waste another class period."

"Oh, God, you're right."

"I know I am."

I bite my lip.

"Call him, Ryan," Josh says as he drops me off in my driveway. "Trust me on this one."

I TAKE JOSH'S ADVICE AND CONTACT BENJI DIRECTLY. I'M too scared to call, so I e-mail him instead, explaining the situation and begging for another chance. I don't know if I'll hear from him at all, but he writes back on Sunday afternoon:

*If you can get the new prints to me by Wednesday, that would be acceptable.*

I walk next door to Josh's house the second I read the e-mail.

He seems surprised to see me.

"Is now a good time?"

"Sure, come in." He holds open the door. I walk into his house, and I'm immediately hit by the smell of the potpourri his mother keeps in dishes around the house: a light fall scent, smooth and slightly sweet, like pine trees. I feel like I'm eight years old again. I remember this house so well.

"You want something to drink?"

"I'm good, thanks."

I stand there for a minute, feeling a bit nostalgic and strange.

"I heard back from Benji," I finally say, after I've soaked up enough of the memory.

"What did he say?"

"I've got until Wednesday to get him two new rolls of prints."

"Can you do it?"

"I hope so," I say. "But I'm nervous. I don't know what to shoot, who to shoot."

"You can do me, if you want."

*You can do me, if you want.* The words play over in my mind. I'd been planning on asking Kimberlee, Mark, my grandparents, maybe. Josh has never crossed my mind.

"You'd be okay with that?" I ask. "It might be kind of weird, since you're in the class and all."

"Of course I'm okay with it." He laughs. "It'd be awfully hypocritical of me to rake you over the coals like that and then not at least offer to help out a little bit. Besides, I'm a photographer too. I know how this stuff works."

My deadline is short and the light is good, so we decide to start right away. There's a large public park down the street from us with a big "natural grass" area. We drive over there in his SUV and wander toward the back, where tall stalks of bamboo are growing wildly.

"Okay, just kind of move around through these," I say, pointing at the bamboo. "Try to act natural." These are terrible directions, the kind of thing an amateur would say, but I'm nervous and he lets me get away with it.

"I'll do my best to be a good model," Josh says, mugging. "I'll make love to the camera."

He's joking, of course, but it makes me feel weird when he says that.

The first couple of frames are a disaster. Josh looks good, but he's posing, and I'm not working around that. If I'm not careful, we're going to wind up with what looks like a headshot for a boy-band audition.

It would be very easy to take a *cute* picture of Josh. Every picture I've ever seen of him is *cute*. His yearbook photos, pics of him playing soccer, casual shots of him at family barbecues or on the beach. It's just not possible for him to look ugly. Ordinarily this is a great problem to have.

But it's killing the film.

Josh's features are boyish, delicate. Large, glassy blue eyes and perfectly clear skin; smooth, shiny brown hair; wide shoulders; toned arms and legs. He's almost too good looking, too pretty.

It's easy to take a great picture of a great-looking person. That's not the point. I need to take an interesting picture, something unexpected. That has always been my focus, my goal. To capture the person in a way that's surprising, raw.

I start breaking down his face, taking close-ups of his ear, his eyes, his jawbone. When you break a human face down like that, it loses some of its meaning, stops being so pretty or handsome.

Studying him this closely through the lens makes me feel

kind of uncomfortable, like it's too personal or something.

It reminds me of lying in bed with Noah, which I did often. We used to take naps together almost every day in the early evenings before my mom got off work. We weren't doing anything sneaky, just sleeping, but if Mom had seen us in bed together, she probably would have freaked out. Noah would always drop off the second his head hit the pillow, but I never did. Sometimes I stayed awake the whole time, just watching him, studying his face while he slept. It was fascinating being close to another human being in that way. Listening to him breathe, in and out, watching his chest rise and fall. I remember tracing the curves of his ear, the outline of his jaw with my fingertip. Seeing his lips moving slightly while he slept, watching his eyelids flutter.

I'm studying Josh's face and body with that kind of intensity now, and it makes me feel weird, like we're lovers or something.

I start experimenting with angles, shooting Josh with his eyes half closed, his chin jutting out, his hair blown sideways by the wind, plastered to his head in a way that's almost ugly. I zoom in on the wrinkles on his forehead as he squints up at the sun.

We stay out there for a long time. When he drops me off

back home, I'm so excited to process the film that I borrow Mark's car and drive over to the photo lab.

It seems to take forever. I'm so impatient to see what I've got that I can barely stand to roll the film, mix the chemicals, let the developer set. But I'm meticulous, and I don't hurry anything. One false step and you can destroy the negatives.

So I hold back, waiting until the timing is exactly right.

And when the film has been processed and dried, when I'm standing in the darkroom watching Josh's face materialize on the blank white paper, I realize that it was worth the wait. They're perfect.

# Freudian Slips

## DR. PAIGE NORRIS, PhD, MD

PATIENT: *Ryan Burke*

PERSONAL GOALS FOR THE WEEK

1. *Do not duck your problems. Confront them.*

# Chapter Seven

MY GUIDANCE COUNSELOR, MS. STACK, PULLS ME out of history class so we can talk about college. I'm annoyed, because this is the day when we pick partners for our big project and I had been hoping to get Josh. Now I will have no say-so in the matter. I will get stuck with whoever is left.

I am also annoyed because I don't like talking about college. The application deadlines are upon me, and I have no idea what I'll do.

"What schools are you applying to, Ryan?"

"Uh . . ." I rattle off a list. I really don't like answering this question. When you're a senior in high school it comes up approximately 8 million times a day. Just last night Grandpa called to harass me about applying to his alma mater, University of Colorado at Boulder. "UGA, University of Texas at Austin, Florida State, UMass."

Ms. Stack stares at me as though I've lost my mind. "That's quite a unique list. I'm not sure I understand your reasoning on all of those choices." She pauses. "Your scores were very, very good. I realize you need to have a couple of safeties—that's always a smart plan—but it sounds to me as though all of your choices are safe schools. Have you considered Duke? Vanderbilt? Some of the Ivies?"

I tell her that I'm still making up my mind. The truth is, I want to go to NYU. I could most likely get in to NYU, maybe land a good scholarship even. But the thought of living in New York terrifies me, and I don't know if I'm ready to take that chance. If I apply and get in, then I'll have to go. There's no way I could come that close and then turn it down.

"I would really encourage you to broaden your scope a bit and apply to some bigger-name universities," she says. "You have the grades, the extracurriculars, and the test scores that will make you an excellent candidate." She stares at me. She can sense that I'm uncomfortable. "Are you worried that you won't get in? Is that it?"

"Kind of," I tell her. And while I'm terrified that I won't get in, there's another part of me—a bigger part, maybe—that's scared I will.

"I have an inspirational quote that you might find helpful." Ms. Stack picks up her notepad and writes something down. Then she tears the page off and hands it to me. It says:

*You miss 100% of the shots you don't take.*

"That's a quote from Wayne Gretzky, the hockey player," she tells me. "Whenever I'm getting discouraged or starting to fear rejection, I think of that."

I nod. "Thank you." I start to rise. "Is it okay if I go back to class now?"

She laughs. "You really are a good student, Ryan. I pull most people out of class and they beg me to keep them longer. Here you are, dying to go back."

"What can I say? I like to learn." It's a joke. I'm actually not some crazy geek who lives for knowledge. But school has always come easily to me. I've never struggled with it the way most people do. And I guess I should be grateful for that, or proud, or something. But I'm not. Most of the time it makes me feel like this giant fraud. Like I got here by accident, like I lucked into some smart gene (probably from my Danny DeVito–look-alike father). Other times, I think back to the whole smart versus pretty argument. You know, when you're a girl, you have to be one or the other.

And I got to be smart, but because of it, I have to be fat.

"You'll consider what I've said?" Ms. Stack asks, as she walks me to the door.

"Yes, I'll think it over."

"Just don't think too long," she warns me. "Deadlines are literally right around the corner."

I promise her that I won't put it off. I don't mean it at the time. I have every intention of putting off this decision for as long as I possibly can.

But I guess her talk stirred me more than I'd like to admit. Because when I get home that night, I print out applications for my three "dream schools": NYU, Vanderbilt, and Brown.

AROUND FOUR O'CLOCK ON MONDAY, KIMBERLEE calls.

"Have you heard 'Girl on Ice'?" she asks anxiously.

"No, I still don't have the CD," I say, annoyed. I've all but given up at this point. *I'll just have to wait and hear it with the rest of the world,* I think sadly.

"Oh."

"What's up?"

"I just saw it."

"You just saw what?" I ask.

"'Girl on Ice.' The video just came on MTV."

"WHAT!"

"It just premiered."

"Right now?"

"Yeah. About five minutes ago." Her voice sounds distant, flat. I can't understand why she's not more excited.

"But it's not supposed to be out for another week!"

"I know. They premiered it early."

"Why didn't you call me?" I demand.

Kimberlee lets out a long breath. "I was pretty shocked. I hit TiVo and I, um, recorded it. And I would have called you, but when I saw the girl come on—"

Oh, my God. "What do you mean?"

She laughs nervously. "You remember that 'Cry Me a River' video Justin Timberlake did a few years ago?"

"Yes." I'm pacing the room now, frantic. I flip on MTV, even though I know the video just played, so it won't be back on for hours.

"Remember how Justin had that Britney look-alike in the video?"

"Yes." I don't like where this is headed.

"There's a . . . girl who looks like you in Noah's video. A lot like you."

I feel my skin go cold. Whenever I hear that someone looks like me, I'm instantly paranoid. I worry that the person will be hugely overweight, or grotesquely ugly, or both. "Is she . . . she's not good looking, is she?"

"It's not that," Kim hedges. "You need to see the video for yourself. Why don't you come over?"

"I'm on my way."

It usually takes me twenty minutes to get to Kimberlee's house. Today, I make it in less than ten. She's waiting by the front door when I get there.

I go charging into the house, making a beeline for the TV.

"Ryan." She holds up a hand to stop me.

"What?"

"Before we watch the video, maybe you'd better take a look at this." Kim hands me a piece of notebook paper.

"What is this?"

"While I was waiting, I sort of went back through the video and wrote down the lyrics . . . the ones I could make out, anyway. So it's not totally accurate, but, uh, you probably ought to read these before you see the video."

I stare at her. "Oh, God. Why?"

"They're kind of . . . disturbing."

"Disturbing how?"

"Even without volume, the video is shocking enough on its own. If you watch it and hear it at the same time." She clenches her teeth. "I was afraid it might be too much."

My cell phone starts ringing. Oh, God. It's that Marilyn woman from the news. I hit the button to send it through to voice mail.

"Why don't you sit down," Kim says, gesturing toward the couch. "I'll get you something to drink."

I pull the Klonopin pills out of my purse while she fetches me a glass of water. I feel on the verge of a panic attack.

With shaking hands, I stare down at the piece of paper. The first line stops me cold, makes me drop my prescription bottle.

*The medication is her friend*

Oh, Christ. I don't know if I can stand to read the rest, but I have to.

*She takes the pills, to mask her sin*
*Her body's known a thousand men*
*She'll leave you at the bitter end*

*She doesn't have a model's grace*
*But she's got such a pretty face*
*It's quite a shame, to watch her trade*
*Her beauty for just one more taste*

*She eats a piece of apple pie*
*Won't slit her wrists, but wants to die*
*Dreams most days of suicide*
*To end this chubby life of lies*

I hear a horrible noise, and for a second I don't even realize that I'm making it. I'm screaming.

Kimberlee comes rushing back. "I told you."

"How?"

"I don't know." She sits down next to me on the couch. "I don't know."

"How could he?"

Kim hugs me.

"He makes me sound like a food-obsessed slut!"

Her eyes lock on mine. She looks horrified. "The bridge is the worst part."

"I didn't even read that far." My hands are shaking.

"You'd better finish it."

I scan down to the bridge.

*Always comes in second place*
*In this, and every single race.*
*Give in, 'cause you know you want her*
*But can you forget their laughter?*
*You try but she won't let you have her*
*And she's moving faster*
*than the one that got away.*

*She is not herself these days*
*Pushes you to go, then stay*
*She slips from sight, she fades away*
*Leaves you broken in her wake*

*Has Daddy issues, left and right*
*Fat is fat, but she denies*
*You try to fight, but love's not blind*
*You let her go, your girl on ice.*

"What the fuck did he do this for?" I ask in a voice near a
whisper. "This isn't me!"

"Of course not."

"Why would he say that? Why would he lie to me? Why would he lie *about* me?"

"I don't know."

"Oh, my God, Kimberlee. I told everyone about this song. My mom, the fucking news! They're all going to think I'm suicidal! Psychotic!"

"I think you should sue him."

"I should, shouldn't I?"

"He libeled you, big-time!"

"Slander," I correct her. "And you're right, he did slander me." Secretly, though, I don't know if I have a case. I *am* fat. I can't disprove that. "But do I have the grounds to prove that he slandered me?"

"Oh, yeah, *chica*. You most certainly do." She's getting steamed now. "'Her body's known a thousand men'? I mean, what the hell is that? You're a virgin, right?"

I nod.

"Then that's defamation or something. Saying you slept with a thousand men? That hurts your character. Big-time."

She's right. "I'm going to call a lawyer." Or maybe my mom can help. She's a paralegal, after all, which is the next best thing.

"Just as soon as you watch the video." Kim grabs the TiVo remote.

"No!" I shriek. "I can't watch it now. I can't . . . I can't see what he thinks of me." I don't like ever knowing what people think of me. I'm happier just pretending like their opinions don't exist.

"I really think you should see it."

"Kim, I can't."

My cell phone's ringing again. This time it's Mom. I ignore it. We can deal with the legal issues later. As soon as it stops ringing, a text message from Josh pops up on the screen. *I just heard your song on the radio. Whoa.*

"Oh, my God, is there anyone in Atlanta who hasn't heard this stupid thing?" I ask.

"Not just Atlanta. It's all over the country," Kim points out unhelpfully.

I glare at her.

"Sorry."

"No, it's not your fault. I'm a ball of nerves." I clutch the Klonopin in my hands. I really want to take one, really need to, but all I can think of is that stupid line from Noah's song. *The medication is her friend.*

"That first part's damaging too," Kim says, as if reading

my mind. "It's like he's saying you're a drug addict." She looks down at the bottle of pills in my hand. "Which isn't even true."

I shut my eyes, willing everything to disappear. I want to be asleep right now, zoned out, high, gone. Anywhere but here.

"We should watch the video."

"Just tell me about it," I say. "I don't want to watch it." My voice is low, soft. All of the sudden, I'm dizzy, exhausted.

"Are you sure?"

"Positive. Just tell me. It'll be easier if I hear it from you."

Kim starts describing the video. "It's got this girl—"

"Is this the girl who looks like me?"

"Yeah. There's only one girl in the video."

I nod. "Go on."

"Okay. There's this girl and she's in this tiny room and she's kind of climbing the walls. And then there's this guy—"

"Is he played by Noah?"

"No, it's some no-name actor."

"Does he look like Noah?"

"Not really."

"So Noah's not in the video at all?"

She sighs. "Really, we should just watch it."

I shake my head. "Continue, please. I'll stop interrupting."

"Noah's in it. It cuts back and forth to concert footage of him playing a guitar onstage, but he's not in the main storyline with the girl. It's kind of like he's narrating the whole thing with his song."

"So what happens with the girl and guy?"

"Right." Kim chews on her lower lip. "The girl is, well, she's dressed in this really ratty, unflattering outfit. And her hair needs to be brushed. And she'd locked up in this tiny room, sort of running around, crashing up against the walls. A little bit like a mental patient, actually."

I cannot watch this video. Not now, maybe not ever.

"And the guy keeps trying to get in and save her. He's holding this picture of the two of them where the girl is made up and looks all pretty—you know, nothing like how she looks now."

I think I'm going to be sick.

"Eventually, at the end of the video, the guy gives up and leaves. Oh!" She snaps her fingers. "And the final scene is of the girl lying very still on the floor of the room. She's all pale and ghostlike, kind of like she's dead. And that's when he sings the title line, 'Girl on Ice.'"

I bury my face in my hands. I sit there for a minute,

shaking. Then something occurs to me. "Is there food in it? He keeps mentioning it in the song."

"Um, yeah. She's sort of, like, eating an apple pie at one point. With her, like, hands. And she's smearing it all over the place."

I'm feeling extremely nauseated now and I get up and make my way to the bathroom.

"Are you okay?" Kimberlee asks, trailing behind me.

"I think I'm—" I'm trying to say, *I think I'm going to be sick*, but I don't get the words out in time. I throw up before I can say them.

KIM OFFERS ME SOME PRESCRIPTION ANTINAUSEA pills—I swear, her house is like a pharmacy—but I decline them in favor of Pepto-Bismol. Once I'm feeling up to it, I drive home, going twenty miles under the speed limit the entire way. It's the exact opposite of how I flew over there.

Once I get home, I crawl into bed.

I'm clutching my cell phone—I want to send Noah a text message.

*Medication is her friend?* I type. *WTF?!?* Once I hit send, I flip the phone off and place it on the desk beside my bed.

You'd think I'd be too keyed up to sleep, but I drift off almost instantly. Whenever I reach rock bottom, I do this. When there's something I need to forget, something I need to avoid, I sleep it off for a few hours. It works miracles.

Unfortunately, I've barely dozed off when my mother comes rushing into my room.

"Oh, Ryan," she says, flopping down on my bed, waking me up. "The girls at work were talking about that awful song! I haven't heard it yet, but they told me what a pack of lies it is!" She puts her arms around me. "How bad is it?"

"I haven't heard it either."

She gasps. "So you didn't know?"

"I sort of knew." I lean over onto the nightstand and fish the piece of paper with the lyrics on it out of my bag. "Here you go."

I lie back, staring up at the ceiling while Mom reads. She keeps making horrified sounds as she goes along. Then, suddenly, she stops. I look at her, and she's calm. "This is all a big misunderstanding," she says, chuckling. "How embarrassing."

"Excuse me?"

"I only wish you hadn't done that interview on the local news," she goes on, "but we'll call Marilyn Roberts and clear it up. Get her to run a retraction. You might come out looking a little silly, but it will be better than the alternative. Which is looking like this." Mom shakes the paper at me.

"Huh?" Maybe it's because I just woke up. But I'm totally confused.

"Obviously," Mom says, crumpling the lyrics in her hands, "this is not the right song."

"What do you mean?"

"You must have gotten confused somehow. This can't be the song Noah wrote about you. It's probably some other track off his album." She pats me on the hand. "No need to worry."

"Maybe you're right." I'm feeling a little better. There's still the matter of the video, but Mom's right. This song doesn't feel like it belongs to me. I don't see how it could.

FOR THE NEXT WEEK MY PHONE RINGS OFF THE hook. I'm deluged with calls from every friend I've ever had (and some I've never had), family members, and that stupid Marilyn Roberts from the local news. I will not talk to her again, though. I couldn't even bring myself to watch myself on the news the first time.

Same way I can't watch the "Girl on Ice" video.

"You're avoiding things," Kim tells me. "You have to face this sometime."

But I disagree. I have avoided many things in my life and, I can honestly say, they do eventually fade off into the distance. You don't have to confront everyone and everything to make it go away. I'm living proof of that.

In the aftermath of the video, I try to get in touch with Noah. I call his cell phone approximately twenty times a day. He never answers and didn't return my text.

But he doesn't change his number.

Every time my phone rings, I hope it will be one of two people—Chelsea or Noah. And I'm always disappointed.

I can't believe Chelsea doesn't try to get in touch with me about the song. She seems totally disinterested in my life, as though she's moved out to the West Coast and dismissed me as her friend in the process.

I try to come up with the reasons why she's doing this. Maybe she's busy. Maybe she doesn't know what to say, how to comfort me. But deep down inside, I think she just doesn't care.

# Freudian Slips

**DR. PAIGE NORRIS, PhD, MD**

PATIENT: *Ryan Burke*

PERSONAL GOALS FOR THE WEEK

1. *Try something before you decide you don't like it.*

# Chapter Eight

WHEN I WAS YOUNGER, I WANTED TO BE anorexic. It was a big goal of mine, because I thought it would solve all my problems. I surfed pro-ana sites and printed off "thinspiration" photos of skeletal supermodels and actresses.

I knew I was playing around where I shouldn't, but I didn't care. I figured I was so far on the other end of the spectrum—morbidly obese—that I could stand to incorporate a few diet tips from the 'rexy squad. After all, these were girls who'd made a lifestyle out of dieting. If I could manage to follow their lead even a small portion of the time, then I was guaranteed to slim down.

This is what I do when I'm stressed. I either eat or I go on a ridiculous diet. Given that "Girl on Ice" has exposed me to the world as a fat chick, I figure I'd better take the second option. My best defense is to get thin. If I'm thin, no one can say the song is about me.

I spend the morning on the elliptical trainer at the Y. I figure it will be a productive way to try to drag my ass out of this slump. Going to the gym is never a fun experience. Oh, afterward, it's pretty all right. Sure, I'm hot and both my hair and clothes are plastered to my body from sweat (I never shower in the company of others—I wait until I get home), but I feel a sense of pride, of accomplishment. As if no matter what else happens, my day is good.

Surprisingly, my least favorite part of working out is the clothes. When I first started going to the gym three years ago, I thought I'd hate the actual exercise most. But, I have to admit, I kind of like it. It makes me feel strong and powerful. When I run, my body gets so loose and light, it's like I'm flying. And I would be flying too, if I didn't have twenty-five pounds of ugly workout clothes weighing me down.

And I do mean ugly.

If you think plus-size evening wear is the worst excuse for fashion on earth, think again. Big girls workout gear (what little of it that exists) is atrocious. Nauseatingly gross. It's all about bad cuts and hot, itchy material that clings in all the wrong places. The pants are too short and too tight—they squeeze your thighs and butt into bound sausages—and the shirts pooch out like maternity wear. And the colors . . . dear

God, the colors! I have one workout jumpsuit in lime green, another in fluorescent blue. It's enough to make me want to give up before I've started.

"WHAT ARE YOU DOING TOMORROW NIGHT?" Kimberlee asks.

Tomorrow's Friday, but I don't have any plans. "Nothing, I guess. What do you have in mind?"

"I have found us the most kick-ass party to attend."

"Who's throwing it?"

"Some guy . . . Todd . . . Tim . . . Tom. I don't remember."

I'm suspicious. "And how do you know about this again?"

"MySpace Events, *chica*!"

Oh, God. Kim has, thankfully, abandoned her plan to look for online dates. Instead, she's taken to befriending college guys on MySpace. She tries to find out all the best events so she can score herself an invitation. "So you don't even know the people who are throwing it?"

"Not yet."

"Then how do you know it will be 'kick-ass'?" I ask.

"Because it's a keg party, frat party, and Halloween party all rolled into one! How could it go wrong?"

I can think of about a million ways, but I remember what

Dr. Paige keeps telling me. Try something before you decide you don't like it. It is my goal for the week, after all.

"What college?"

"UGA!"

UGA is University of Georgia at Athens. It's a great college town, but it's a bit of a haul from here. Especially if we're going to be drinking.

"You want to drive all the way down to Athens and back just for some party that may or may not be any fun?"

"Oh, it'll be fun. Trust me," says Kim. "All the best, hottest frat boys are going to be there. And there will be free drinks! We can get totally plastered!"

"And then drive drunk all the way home? I don't think so."

"Hmm, good point." She mulls this over. "So we won't drink. Or I won't drink since I'll be the one driving."

I think it over. "I don't know. If I didn't have to get up early Saturday. And if it weren't a Halloween party, I'd be more up for going."

"You don't like Halloween?" she asks, astonished.

"No, I don't like Halloween."

Actually, this is an understatement.

I hate Halloween.

Okay, okay . . . so I don't totally hate it. I'm not that big of a stick in the mud.

There are a lot of things about Halloween that I love.

I like horror movies, and pumpkin carving, and haunted houses. What I hate is the costumes. Finding regular clothes that make me look good is challenging enough; now imagine how tough it is to find a trendy plus-size costume. Making matters worse, all of the skinny chicks take the opportunity to show off their hot bods in some rocking costume or another. Nothing shatters my self-esteem like standing around in a dowdy, floor-length witch's robe while all the cute girls parade around as French maids, belly dancers, and leotard-clad devils.

"Why don't you like Halloween?"

"Because I can never find a costume I like."

"We can get you something cute," she assures me. "I'm terrific when it comes to planning Halloween costumes. Last year I went to this awesome party and my costume was the biggest hit of the night."

"What did you dress up as?"

"That *Tomb Raider* chick."

My point exactly. "Something tells me a costume like that wouldn't look too great on me."

"Oh, don't be silly. We'll get you a costume that's just as hot. I already have my outfit picked out, so I can devote one hundred percent of my energy to helping you find something great."

"You already have your costume?"

"Yeah. I bought it last November, when all the Halloween stuff was on clearance."

"What is it?"

"A naughty nurse . . . it's so f'ing sexy, I can't stand it."

Yet again, she's proved my point.

But I need to get out of my shell some, so I agree to go.

"I was thinking . . . we don't have much time, but I bet we could rig you up a witch's costume that would look really good," Kimberlee says.

Basic black, I liked it. "Yes," I reply. "I bet we could." I had been a witch a dozen times before—what was once more?

"Awesome! I'll come over tomorrow after school and we can get ready."

A HOT GUY IS TALKING TO ME. THIS NEVER HAPPENS, and I don't know how to react.

"I hope this isn't weird," he says, perching on the armrest next to me. He's dressed as a pirate and he's wearing an open shirt that shows off his buff chest. "But I saw you across the room and wanted to come say hi."

He thinks I'm someone else. His sister's college roommate. A long-lost friend. He's got me confused with some other plus-size witch. My costume is actually pretty cool. Kim helped me with it. I was going to go as just a regular, garden-variety witch. But she insisted I wear something tighter, a bit more low-cut, with major cleavage.

"We don't . . . I'm pretty sure we don't know each other," I tell him.

He bursts out laughing. "We do now." He extends his hand. "I'm Jared."

"Ryan," I say, taking his hand. His handshake is firm, and he grips my fingers for a second longer than he should.

"Ryan?" he repeats.

I nod.

"That's such a cool name."

"Thanks."

He hands me a Miller Lite, and I crack the can open.

"Do you go to UGA?"

"No," I tell him, sipping the beer. "I'm a senior at Greenlee High." As soon as the words leave my mouth, I regret them. I've completely blown our cover. We're supposed to be juniors from Georgia Tech. Twenty-one years old. Not jailbait, not underage drinkers. You can sleep with us, serve us beer, and the cops won't break down your door.

"Wow." Jared arches an eyebrow. "You're young."

"I'm eighteen," I improvise, trying to save the situation.

"Cool." He looks around the room. "You come here with anyone?"

"My friend Kim," I tell him. "She goes to Georgia Tech. She's a junior there. A communications major," I say. I'm overdoing it. The sure sign of a liar is that they volunteer more information than is necessary. Fortunately, Jared doesn't seem to be paying close attention.

"No boyfriend?" he asks, giving me a little wink.

"Nope."

"Good." He slides off the armrest, landing on the couch beside me. Our legs are touching. "Not that I'm afraid of a little competition. But it's nice to have you all alone." I like the way he cuts to the chase. I guess that kind of confidence comes naturally when you're good looking.

"Yeah, it is," I say, and freeze.

All my life, I've been waiting for this. I've been waiting to get thin so the hot boys of the world would crawl out of the woodwork, line up. Now, here one is, and I have no idea what to do. I never expected this to happen while I was still fat.

I look up and see Kimberlee standing about ten feet away. She's flanked by a group of frat boys, but she's frantically trying to catch my attention. We lock eyes, and she gives me a thumbs-up.

"Where are you going to college next year?" Jared asks, gulping his beer. "Staying in state?"

"Nah, I'd really like to go to Tisch—the arts school at NYU. They have a great photography program."

"So you're a photographer?" he asks.

"Kind of." I take a swig of Miller Lite.

"You're just being modest. I bet you're great!"

"I'm okay. My parents—my mother—wants me to go to Emory and major in business. Or go to Vanderbilt."

"Vandy's nice," Jared says. "I have a few friends there." He scoots closer to me. "I'm majoring in French." The way he's looking at me, I almost expect him to add "kissing" to the end of the sentence, but thank God he doesn't. "I want to move to Paris one day," he says, running his fingers along the side of my face, "to teach."

"That's a, um, great goal."

We finish our round of beers and he fetches two more, then sits back down beside me.

"So are you going to pledge when you get to college?"

"I haven't decided yet," I tell him. This is the truth. On the one hand, I've never seen myself as the sorority type. Then again, it could be really fun. I love the idea of instant best friends, a full social calendar—never having to worry about what you're going to do on a Friday or Saturday night.

"What house?"

I am totally lost here. I know they all have Greek letters, but the truth is, all the deltas and the alphas and the gammas run together. I do remember one of Mark's ex-girlfriends was really into Alpha Delta Pi. She couldn't wait to get to Auburn so she could pledge there.

"Maybe Alpha Delta Pi," I say. "But we'll see."

He seems impressed. "Chi O's a good one too," he says.

Jared and I talk for a little while longer. I'm not sure how much time passes. We make it through two more rounds of beers, and by this point I'm feeling downright tipsy.

I can feel him staring at me and I think that if I turn my head he might lean in and kiss me. I don't know what to do. *Make a move or sit still, make a move or sit still . . .* This seems to be the ongoing theme of my life. Although, really, I don't even have to do much. I just have to sit there and let it happen. I just have to turn my face. It's not like I'm risking rejection. But my body feels frozen, and I can't do it.

"So Ryan . . . ," he says. "Do you want to go outside for a bit? It's so loud in here."

*If I go outside, he will kiss me.* I nod. We stand up and go and, a few minutes later, we're in front of the house. I'd forgotten how cold it is tonight and I shiver. The cold always surprises me. It's warm most of the year in Hotlanta, which got its nickname for a reason.

"I have a jacket in the car," Jared offers. "You want me to go get it?"

"No thanks," I say abruptly. He's so thin, I doubt it will fit me. And that would be an embarrassing moment.

"You sure?"

"I like being cold," I tell him. "It makes me feel alive." Oh. My. God. Of all the cheesy things to say!

"You know what makes me feel alive?" he asks, moving in closer. I brace myself for it. "This." He leans in, putting his arm around my waist and moving me toward him. One second we're apart, and the next we're kissing.

I've never been a big fan of kissing. Most guys are too

aggressive, too rough. They open their mouth too wide, propel their tongue at you like a battering ram. And there's nothing soft or romantic or even remotely arousing about it.

But Jared is different. *Better.* He kisses the way I've always wanted. Gentle, tender. It feels incredible.

We break apart a minute later and then kiss again, briefly this time. His cell phone starts ringing in the middle of it and he brings it to his mouth to answer.

"Ashley!" he says, sounding excited.

*Ashley can be a guy's name, right?*

"What are you up to?"

He takes a few steps away and turns his back toward me.

"I've been thinking about you."

*Crap. Crap. Crap.*

"You want to come over here? Yeah, let me give you directions." Jared walks away until he's out of earshot. A minute later, he comes back. "I've got to go pick up my friend," he says apologetically. "I'm sorry."

"Will you be back?" I ask hopefully.

"Maybe," he hedges, and I can read the subtext. *Sorry to kiss and run. You were nice to pass the time with, but I've got a better girl—a hotter girl—to hook up with now. Game over.*

"Well, it was nice meeting you," I say, and then think better of it. I'm not going to let this go so easily. I'm not going to just drop it and move on, which is what I always do. Time to get a little bolder. "Can I see your phone for a sec?"

Jared eyes me quizzically, then hands it over. I go to his address book and key in my name and number. "I put my cell number in there," I say. "Call me sometime."

"Okay," he says, heading off. "See ya, Ryan."

The beer must be making me bolder, because I lean in and kiss him on his smooth, hairless cheek. "I sure hope so," I whisper in his ear.

He hugs me briefly. "Take care."

And then he's gone. Just like that. I watch him walk off down the sidewalk, past the endless line of cars, and disappear into the night. All at once I feel terribly sad, like a kid the day after Christmas when the tree's been taken down and the gifts have all been unwrapped and the only thing remaining is a pile of crumpled paper and the knowledge that you've got 364 more days before this gets here again.

I've kissed three other guys in my entire life. Three. And none of them even came close to kissing as well as Jared. And, yet, I don't know anything about him. Sure, I gave him my number, but I didn't bother to get his. Who knows if I'll ever see him again?

Maybe getting what you want isn't so great after all. 'Cause getting it doesn't always mean keeping it.

I walk back into the party to search for Kimberlee. I'm dying to tell her about the kiss, get her opinion on it.

My cell phone's going off, signaling that I have a text message. When I see who it's from, I stop dead in my tracks. Noah.

*Everybody takes pills, what do u care? It's not a big deal.*

*What do I care?* I write him back. *You shouldn't broadcast that!*

Given how long it took him to reply to my first message, I don't expect to hear back. But my cell starts buzzing again before I can even find Kimberlee.

*Nobody knows who the lyrics r about.*

I grimace. More people than you think. I spy Kim and rush over. I quickly fill her in on Noah and show her the text messages.

"That sucks," she says. "I can't believe he's so blasé. What an ass!"

"I know!"

We talk about it for a minute longer, then she notices that I'm alone.

"Where's Jared?" she asks.

"He left."

"Is he coming back?"

"Hey, wait a minute." I place my hand on Kim's arm. "How did you know his name? I never introduced you."

"Tom." She points to the guy at her left. "They're buddies."

"Jared's a good guy," Tom says, turning to face me.

"So where did he go?" Kim asks.

"To pick up someone named Ashley."

"Oh," Tom says.

"Oh." Kim cringes, giving me a sympathetic look.

"What?" I ask. "Is that his girlfriend or something?"

They exchange glances. "A little bit," Kim says, putting her hand on my shoulder. "I'm so sorry."

"He wishes," Tom clarifies. "He's been chasing that girl for years."

"Looks like he finally got her," I mumble.

"What?"

"Nothing."

"So, did you guys hook up?" Kim whispers, leaning in close.

"I'll tell you later. Do you mind if we get out of here?"

"Sure," she says, putting her arm around me. "Let's go catch a movie or something. My treat." She grins.

We start toward the door. "Wait, you guys are leaving?" Tom asks, looking startled. "But you only just got here!"

"We've seen all we need to see," Kim says. "This party sucks. They don't even have kegs—just canned shit. What kind of keg party doesn't have kegs?" She makes a face.

"You guys drove all the way from Atlanta just to stay for five minutes?"

Tom has a point. But I don't want to hang around to watch Jared come back with his pseudo-girlfriend.

"It's been more than five minutes," Kim tells him.

"Ah, come on," Tom pleads. "You don't have to go *right this second.*"

Kim hesitates. She looks like she wants to stay, but she's trying to be a loyal friend. "I'm sorry, but we've really got to get going."

"It's okay," I jump in. "We can hang out for a little longer." This isn't that big a deal. I shouldn't let Jared ruin my entire night.

"Then it's decided!" Tom says, handing Kim another beer. "You guys can hang out for a while."

"Of course we can!" I say, a little too enthusiastically.

Kim looks at me. "Are you sure?" she whispers.

"Totally." I force a smile.

"Okay, one drink and then we're going," she tells Tom. She passes her beer over to me. "But I think I'd better make it a bottled water. Designated driver and all that." He goes to fetch her one.

"Are you sure you're okay with staying?" she asks. "You looked pretty upset a few minutes ago."

"I'll be all right," I tell her.

She gives me a hug. "Thanks, Ryan. The second you feel uncomfortable, let me know, and we'll bolt."

One drink has a way of turning into three or four, so we wind up hanging out longer. I've loosened up, put Jared out of my mind as much as possible, when it happens. I'm standing with Kim, Tom, and a few other people when he shows back up. It's about an hour later. I wonder how far he had to drive to get this girl. At first I don't see anyone with him, but a minute later, a gorgeous, fair-skinned brunette slips her arm through his. If this is Ashley—and it's got to be—then I'm screwed. She's gorgeous. Skinny. Really, really skinny.

Fuck.

"That's Ashley," Tom says. "She hot as hell, huh?" I want to smack him and tell him to shut up. But I don't. I try to act is if I couldn't care less.

"Uh-huh." I lean my head back and take a huge swig of beer. "She's a little hottie." I hate the way girls are always expected to do this. If we don't compliment another chick on her appearance, we're jealous. Yet, guys never have to give props to other guys. It's annoying.

"She's all right," Kimberlee says. "A little skanky, though."

"Skanky?" Tom shakes his head. "That girl is fine as hell! I heard she turned down a spot with the Pussycat Dolls so she could finish her education."

Kim bursts out laughing. "No way. Her boobs aren't nearly big enough."

"You're just jealous," Tom says, looking annoyed. "Jared is one lucky MF if you ask me."

"I thought you said they weren't together?" I ask, trying to sound casual. I'm hoping he'll get rejected, come crawling back to me. Pathetic, huh?

"She wants him when she's horny," Tom tells us. "They sleep together all the time, but he wants to be more than some easy lay. Poor Jared's so in love with the girl, he can't see straight." He laughs, drinks his beer. "Me, I'd just go for the sex and be done with it."

I look over at them, and Jared's got his arms around her, he's nuzzling her neck, the side of her face. This makes me feel kind of sick, so I go outside to get some fresh air. Kim runs after me.

"I'm sorry, *chica*," she says. "It just wasn't meant to be. He's taken."

"Which absolutely sucks."

"I'm sorry nothing happened. I know you liked him."

"I *kissed* him."

She grins. "You *did*? That's awesome!"

"It was for about a minute." I kick a piece of gravel with my shoe. "Until his girlfriend showed up."

"Let's go," Kim says, taking my hand.

We find her car, which is approximately a hundred blocks away. "I don't remember it being this far," I say as we hoof it down the sidewalk.

"God, don't say things like that." She looks alarmed. "I'm already paranoid enough about the thing being stolen." Right then, she spies her Mercedes.

We make it back to Atlanta in just under an hour. As we're nearing the home stretch, Kimberlee steers the car off the highway and into the parking lot of a small twenty-four-hour diner.

"I don't feel like going home yet, and it's too late for a movie. I thought we could grab something to eat."

"That sounds great," I say. I don't feel like going home

either. And after my bum night with Jared, I feel like I deserve a little treat to cheer me up.

"This place has the best waffles in the entire state of Georgia. My mom used to take us here when we were on road trips."

We go inside, sit down, and order. Kimberlee gets practically everything on the menu: waffle, french fries, scrambled eggs with cheese, bacon, coffee.

I get a small waffle and a large Diet Coke.

"You'll never eat all that," the waitress says to Kim.

"Oh, try me!" she laughs. "I'm freaking starving. I haven't eaten anything today."

We talk about school, Taylor, Kim's workout routine for dance squad. She steers clear of Noah and Jared.

The food comes, and she digs in. True to her word, she manages to eat most of it, which amazes me. "I don't know how you can do that and stay so thin," I say wistfully. We never talk about weight. I don't like bringing it up; I figure she can't understand.

"I work out, like, all the time," she says. "You should come with me."

This actually sounds like a good plan. Perhaps that's what I need. A workout buddy; someone who will kick my ass into shape. "Let's do it!" I say, perking up. "When can you go?"

"How about tomorrow morning?"

"I have photography class."

"Oh, that's right. What time do you have to be there again?"

"Seven sharp," I remind her.

She gulps her coffee. "That's insane."

"That's when the best light is."

"So how's the class going?"

"Pretty well." I tell her about shooting Josh at the park. She seems excited for me. We talk about photography for a while, and then the conversation switches to clothes. I struggle to keep up as Kim talks about the Louis Vuitton bag and Stella McCartney boots she's getting. But my mind keeps drifting off to Jared. It sounds hokey, I know, but I really thought he was The One. Not as in The One I'm Supposed to Marry or anything crazy like that. I never expected us to become boyfriend and girlfriend. But he was my first hot guy. Doesn't every girl, by law of nature, get to hook up with an insanely hot guy at least once in her life? Even if it doesn't last?

I tune back in to the conversation in time to hear Kim say how unhappy she is with her hair. She wants it "Gwen Stefani blond."

"Your hair looks great," I assure her. "Your *everything* looks great. Your body is absolutely perfect."

"Thanks." She smiles. "But I'd like to be known for something else. The pretty thing—it gets old, you know."

Oh, my God, she's not going *there*, is she? I hate to sound bitter, but why do pretty girls always do this? Why do they always pretend like being drop-dead gorgeous is a burden and that life would be so much easier if they were ugly?

I tell her this.

"No . . . I'm not trying to sound ungrateful. I know I've got a good thing going." She chomps on a fry. "But when you hear anything a bunch, it loses its meaning. I'm tired of everyone thinking I'm just 'the pretty girl.' It's like with Noah's song—"

"Oh, God! Please don't bring that up."

"No, no, no . . . hear me out. Despite what people are saying, you should be really happy about it. *Noah Fairbanks* took the time to write a song about you!" She offers me a fry, and I push it away.

"A song that makes me look like a suicidal, food-obsessed freak."

"It's not like that's what everyone thinks. And if they do,

they're just jealous. They just wish Noah cared enough to write a song about them."

"I guess so."

"It's an honor, if you think about it."

She's trying to be nice, but all I can think is, *If I were thin, none of this would have happened.*

W E DON'T GET HOME UNTIL ALMOST THREE a.m. I'm barely awake when Josh arrives the next morning to pick me up at 6:45. We've decided to start riding together, since it makes sense.

"I'm sorry I'm late," he says. "I figured you'd want a few extra minutes to sleep after your big party last night."

I hop up into the SUV.

"Oh, I ran through Starbucks," he says, handing me an iced mocha.

Wow, that was nice of him.

"Thanks!" I say, grateful for the caffeine rush. "What do I owe you?"

"Don't worry about it."

On the way to class, I fill him in on the previous night. I tell him about Jared, mentioning the kiss but not dwelling on it. I don't want to sound needy and pathetic, even though I kind of am right now. Pining over a five-minute hookup screams loser.

"Sounds like you had an awesome time."

"Great." I sip my coffee.

"What time did you get home?"

"After three."

Josh says, "I figured you'd be out pretty late."

"That's Kim for you."

He laughs. "Yeah, she's a handful."

We get to class without a second to spare. Benji's pacing the room, looking irritated. He always looks irritated.

"Do you want to roll with me today?" Josh whispers as we sit down.

"Sure."

Since most of the other students are still working on prints from last week, Josh and I have the rolling room to ourselves. We grope past the curtain, our hands feeling along the black walls.

We talk animatedly while we work. Josh really loves my latest prints, and he tells me so.

"That's just because you're the subject," I tease him.

"Even so," he says. "I think they really rock."

As luck would have it, Benji agrees.

"Ms. Burke," he says, eyeing me with approval. "I have some excellent news for you. From worst to best." He holds up my pictures of Josh.

"Are you guys dating?" Gwen Landry asks.

I start to open my mouth to tell her no, when Benji interjects. "Let's stay on the topic at hand. No childish gossip *please*."

I never get to answer. And all through class, everyone's looking at us, looking at me, like they know that we're together.

And I have to admit, it feels kind of nice.

# Freudian Slips

## DR. PAIGE NORRIS, PhD, MD

PATIENT: *Ryan Burke*

PERSONAL GOALS FOR THE WEEK

1. *Keep track of your "weird food behavior."*

# Chapter Nine

"**I**F I WERE THIN, HE WOULD HAVE CALLED."

"Who would have called?" Kimberlee asks. It's the following week, and we're sitting in her bedroom, drinking smoothies and watching *Grey's Anatomy* on DVD.

"Jared," I say, sucking a crushed-up hunk of pineapple through my straw. "If I were thin, Jared would have called."

She turns to face me, looking utterly confused. "Who's Jared?"

"The guy I met at the Halloween party we went to! How can you not remember that?"

"'Cause, it was, like, a lifetime ago, *chica.*"

"Yeah, but he's still on my mind. . . ."

"Why are you worried about that Jared guy? You've got Josh now."

"First of all," I say, fighting back a blush, "I do not *have* Josh. Megan does."

"For the time being. I saw your photos of him, remember? He was looking at the camera like he loooved you. Besides, Megan's a bitch," Kim says. "She's also kind of a slut. She's never faithful to her boyfriends. Sooner or later, Josh will figure that out and move on."

"Yeah, but he won't move on to me."

"Not if your attitude stays like that," Kim says, sounding annoyed. "I'm not trying to be rude, Ryan, but you've got to stop being so negative. You're always predicting things will turn out for the worst. You have to go with the flow, relax a little." I'm about to respond, when she snaps her fingers. "Was Jared the pirate?"

"Yes."

"I totally remember him." She grins. "He was hot."

"Thanks for reminding me," I say sarcastically.

"Be excited!" Kim thumps me on the arm. "Didn't you guys kiss?"

"Yes. For about five seconds."

"So? Didn't you say he was a great kisser?"

"He was," I admit.

"That's awesome." She's beaming from ear to ear. "Why aren't you happier?"

"Because, I got to hook up with Jared for this brief,

fleeting moment. And then he took my number but never called."

Kim shrugs. "It happens."

"To me it happens," I say, a lump forming in my throat. "It wouldn't have happened to you." She starts to object, but I stop her. "If I were thin, he would have called." I can't resist saying it again.

She stirs her smoothie with a straw. "No, he wouldn't have. He wouldn't have called if you were thin."

"Okay, if I were thin *and* gorgeous, *then* he would have called."

Kim sets down her drink and rolls over onto one side, propping herself up on one elbow. "He's in love with that other girl, remember? The one dressed up in the cat costume? You weren't going to be able to get in the middle and bust that up."

"If I looked different, I could have," I tell her. "I could have competed."

"It's not always a competition. And looks aren't everything. They really aren't. They don't guarantee you some perfect life."

I'm starting to get exasperated. I don't want to be like this, but I can't help it. "People like you—beautiful people— always say things like that. You're always saying that looks don't matter. But you should try being like me for a few days. You'd see how it works then."

"And you should try being me."

"I wish I could."

"Seriously. I don't get what I want all of the time."

"Just ninety-nine-point-nine percent of the time, right?" I tease.

"Ryan." Kim rolls her eyes. "It doesn't work that way. Being thin doesn't make you some superhero. You don't always save the day, get the guy."

"Yeah, but come on," I argue. "If I looked different, Jared wouldn't have gone running off to Ashley."

"Sure, he would have."

"But if I were prettier than she is . . ."

Kimberlee drums her fingers on the tabletop. "It wouldn't have mattered. Think about Kerry Vance and Ava Peeler. Pretty doesn't always win."

Kerry Vance and Ava Peeler are two seniors at Greenlee High. Last year they got into a heated fight over one of the hottest guys in school, a track-and-fielder named Brian Marsh. The funny thing was, everyone assumed Kerry would win hands down. Kerry was blond and perky and gorgeous. Captain of the volleyball team, president of the dance squad—she looked like she'd stepped off the cover of *Maxim*. Ava was considerably less attractive. She was short and scrawny, with big teeth and frizzy brown hair. She was average at best. Where Kerry was cute and sexy, Ava was babyish and dorky. She wore her hair in messy ponytails, carried around a stuffed koala bear, and drew sloppy henna tattoos on her hands during class.

And, yet, Brian picked Ava. Kerry was mortified—the rest of us were just plain shocked. You don't see something like that happen every day. But here's the thing: If I had been in Ava's position, I would have dropped out of the race the second I saw my competition. I would have assumed, as all of us did, that Kerry was going to come out the victor.

I guess this is what my guidance counselor, Ms. Stacks, meant when she gave me that Wayne Gretzky quote, *You miss 100% of the shots you don't take.*

The words run through my mind. Even if you fail 99 percent of the time, wouldn't you rather have that 1 percent of success? Wouldn't it be worth it?

Maybe that's what Ava did. I'd known people like her before. People who, outwardly at least, didn't seem to have that much going for them. But they came out on top, again and again.

I just assumed they were lucky, that things came easily to them. But how could I really know for sure? Success is usually so public, whereas failure tends to be more private. No guy's going to go around boasting about the twenty hot girls who rejected him. He's going to show off the one who said yes.

*How often have you actually tried and failed, Ryan? I ask myself. Versus the number of times you've just assumed you'd fail. You think you know everything that will happen, but that's impossible. You've had one or two bad experiences, and they scarred you so much that you retreated into your shell and never came back out. People don't behave in the ways that feel good to them; they behave in ways that are familiar. You keep repeating the same patterns over, expecting to get different results. And when you don't, you assume you failed because of your weight.*

"Look, there's something I didn't tell you," Kimberlee says. "It's about the Halloween Party."

For a moment I have a sick feeling in the pit of my stomach. I'm afraid she's going to say she put Jared up to kissing me or something equally awful.

"You remember Tom? That guy I was talking to at the party?"

"Of course."

203

"I didn't exactly win him over."

"What do you mean?"

"I tried to come on to him when you were outside with Jared, and he pushed me away."

I stare at her. "That's crazy."

Kim smiles. "I was the one who insisted we drive down to Athens for that stupid party, and then nobody was interested in me. And you hooked up with one of the hottest guys there."

"How did he reject you?" I ask.

"I asked him if he wanted to go outside and 'talk' in my car," Kim explains, "And he said, 'We can talk right here.' So I said, 'But we can't make out right here.'" She grimaces. "And he replied, 'No thanks.'"

"Ouch!" I can't believe she didn't take off after that, just stood there and smiled and talked to Tom like it was no big deal.

"Tell me about it."

She's so gorgeous, and Tom was so plain. It didn't make sense. "He was flirting with you all night. Do you know why he wasn't interested?"

"No idea. It just happens that way sometimes."

"But I figured girls like you . . ."

"Girls like me? Trust me, *chica*, we get rejected too."

"But it seems like everyone else is having more fun than I am," I complain. "They always come in with these wild stories about what they did last weekend. Meanwhile, I sat at home and watched TiVo."

"You don't know how often they're telling the truth. Most people's lives are far less glamorous than you probably imagine."

**From:** chels_bells89@hotmail.com (Chelsea Ramsay)

**To:** inthegutterlookingathestars@photo.lx (Ryan Burke)

**Sent:** Friday, November 17, 2006 9:13 P.M.

**Subject:** I'll be back for the new semester

Cheer up! It's only another month and then my plane will be touching down in Hotlanta. And I'll be back home for good . . . or at least until college starts in the fall. The important thing is, I'll be there for prom and spring break and graduation and all that other awesome stuff I wouldn't miss for anything in the world.

I know our friendship has been a little strained with me being gone for so long. But, as painful as it was, I had to do this. I had to spend this time here in California, with my dad. You know how awful our relationship has always been. But I think things are getting better. I think me being here for the past couple of months has kind of mellowed out his colossal jerkiness. If you can believe that! Anyway, I'll fill you in on all the details when I get home.

—Chels

I can't believe it! Only one month until my best friend is back.

I'm a little nervous about seeing her, to tell you the truth. You know how things get when you're away for a while . . . you get out of step with each other. Plus, I've been spending so much time with Kimberlee lately, and I'm worried how the two of them will get along. *If* they'll get along.

But I can't stress about that now. At the moment, I'm only feeling happy. Chelsea will be back, for definite, for good.

I pull out my calendar and mark the date.

MY WEIRD FOOD BEHAVIOR

*1. At restaurants, I always order more food than I can possibly eat. I have this irrational*

*fear that if I don't get a large portion, then I'll*
*"run out before I'm full!"*
2. *I feel very possessive of my food.*
*I get upset if people try to eat something*
*that is mine.*
3. *When sharing a pizza, I obsess about*
*whether other people will "steal" all the*
*slices before I've had enough.*
4. *I find it difficult to be in a room where*
*other people are eating and I'm not.*
5. *If I really desire a certain snack—*
*a Snickers bar, a piece of cake, whatever—*
*it's better for me to go ahead and eat it right*
*away. Otherwise, I will be consumed*
*with thoughts of it all day.*
6. *I can't be around food without*
*wanting to eat it.*
7. *I spend an awful lot of time*
*(read: most of the day) thinking about*
*(a) what I am going to eat or*
*(b) what I have just eaten.*

# Freudian Slips

## DR. PAIGE NORRIS, PhD, MD

PATIENT: *Ryan Burke*

PERSONAL GOALS FOR THE WEEK

1. Compile a list of five ways your weight protects you.

# Chapter Ten

JOSH HAS STARTED CALLING ME. AT FIRST IT WASN'T a big deal—he'd call me every day or so to ask a question about history class or to make a comment on Benji McGann. We'd only talk for a minute, maybe five. And then we'd hang up. But lately the calls have started to feel different. I've gotten the sense that his little questions are just a ruse—that's he's really looking for a casual way to start a conversation.

Tonight, for instance, he calls to ask how many rolls of film we were supposed to shoot for this weekend's photo class. A silly question, since Benji's assignments come in a pattern. We started out with two, and each week we've added an additional roll. Josh knows this; he takes better notes than anyone.

Still, he calls my cell to ask.

"Uh, one more than last week," I tease him. "Same as always."

"Sorry, I got confused."

"Anyway . . ." I let my voice trail off.

"And we're doing two color rolls?"

"Uh-huh."

"C forty-one, right? 'Cause we can't get the others processed."

"Josh Lancaster, don't even try to pretend you don't know that," I scold him playfully, as I kick off my shoes and climb onto my bed. It's after ten o'clock, and I'm planning to go to sleep soon. "It's Photography 101. Next thing I know, you'll be asking me to explain what a thirty-five millimeter camera is."

He laughs. "Well, now that you mention it . . . I was going to get you to explain point-and-shoot to me."

"Very funny."

We joke about cameras for another minute, and then the conversation shifts.

"What are you planning to do next year?" he asks.

"Next year?"

"Yeah, college. I know you've got it all figured out."

"I so do *not* have it all figured out." I sigh. "Why does everyone think that?"

"You seem pretty focused," he says, "pretty organized. I figured you filled out your apps months ago."

"Well . . . I'm still deciding."

"Between?"

"NYU, Vandy . . . a few other places. Maybe UGA," I throw in.

"UGA?" he asks. "You don't want to leave the state?"

"I don't know," I hedge. "It's so hard to decide. What about you?"

"Oh, damn!" he laughs. "I thought you knew. I'm going to Columbia. Early acceptance."

"Columbia? Fuck, that's impressive."

"Thanks."

I balance the phone against my ear. "And early acceptance . . . jeez, no nail-biter for you."

"Thank God for that." He sounds relieved. "I'm way too high-strung to wait. I'd have lost my mind if I hadn't heard anything back yet."

"*You're* high-strung?" I ask.

"Oh, God, yes."

There's a tone in his voice, something I'm not used to hearing.

"But you always seem so laid-back."

"*Seeming* and *being* are two different things."

"I guess so."

"I worry a lot," he admits. "All the time."

"About what?" What in the world could Josh Lancaster have to worry about?

"My career. Getting older. Family stuff . . . my dad and I don't always get along so well. He used to drink a lot . . . it's better now, 'cause he's in AA. But there were some pretty rough years."

Whoa. I never knew this. "I'm so sorry. I had no idea."

"Most people don't . . . most people don't really want to hear about that kind of stuff. You know how it is. I'm the happy-go-lucky guy at school. It's easier that way, I guess."

He sounds strange, unsure of himself almost. I feel so stupid and naive. Why have I believed all this time that people like Josh and Kimberlee had it perfect? How could I have been this dense?

We talk for two more hours, and the time flies by. He tells me more about his family life, about how tough it's been growing up with an alcoholic father. It's weird that I never knew this. Then again, the last time I really hung out next door I was ten years old. And I was too busy playing Xbox with Josh to notice that Mr. Lancaster was lacing his Saturday morning coffee with bourbon.

Josh's confession makes me relax, open up to him. For the

moment, at least, we can tell each other anything. I know this feeling will fade—we're enjoying that strange intimacy that exists only during late-night phone calls—so I take advantage of it while it lasts.

I tell Josh about my mom and Mark, about my strained friendship with Chelsea, my insecurities with guys. It's comforting, somehow, sharing these things with Josh, having him listen. I feel really close to him, which is weird, because on the outside we're totally different.

I go to bed feeling strange, tingly almost.

But by the next morning, when I get to school, the magic has evaporated. He's just the same old Josh Lancaster, hanging out with Megan before the bell rings, goofing around with his soccer buddies, Big Man on Campus without a care in the world.

We pass each other in the hallway before homeroom.

He nods hello to me, but he doesn't stop to talk.

THIS WEEK I HAVE TO LIST FIVE WAYS MY WEIGHT IS protecting me. Dr. Paige is very big on this theme. She believes I wear my fat like a suit of armor. She thinks I use it as a way to keep people at arm's length.

I think she's crazy.

"Your weight makes you feel invisible," she said last week. "And feeling invisible gives you the illusion of being safe."

"That doesn't make any sense," I argued back. "If I wanted to be invisible, then wouldn't I waste away, starve myself down until I was eighty pounds? Why would I make myself bigger? My size guarantees that I get noticed. It makes it impossible for me to blend into the background. Everyone sees me. Everyone."

"Ah, yes," she replied. "But they don't really see you, not in any ways that are scary or uncomfortable."

"I'm not following."

"They don't see you as a sexual object, for example. You don't get a lot of sexual attention from men."

That stopped me cold. It wasn't that I thought she was right; I just didn't know how to respond. Of course I wasn't a sexual object. But, whoa boy, did I want to be one. Yes, yes, yes! I did! I wanted to be like Kimberlee Johnston. Perfect body, lots of boys, lots of sex. Didn't I?

"Your weight keeps you isolated," she went on. "And while on some levels you're sad about that, on others you're relieved."

"It's like you're saying I want to be fat," I said. "Which is ludicrous."

"I think there's a part of you that wants to be fat, yes," she said. "Although I don't know if 'want' is actually the right word choice. What's more accurate is that I think you're afraid of being thin. You're afraid of how your life will change if that happens. You'll have to face some uncomfortable truths about the world. Not to mention some uncomfortable situations."

There was an awkward silence. Fortunately, my fifty minutes was almost up, so Dr. Paige wrote out the assignment—five ways your weight protects you—and let me go.

I had never been so glad to get out of there.

Now here I sit in my bedroom, with a notebook spread out in front of me. I've been trying to come up with my list for twenty minutes, but so far no dice. I've got to get this finished tonight since my appointment with her is tomorrow afternoon.

After another twenty minutes of nothing, I pick up the phone and call Chelsea long distance. I'm hoping she can help. Or, at the very least, she'll be able to make fun of Dr. Paige with me.

Chelsea has been a little bit better about keeping in touch over the past week. Maybe it's because she misses our friendship.

But the cynical part of me thinks it's because Christmas break is right around the corner, and she'll be coming back to Atlanta. She probably wants to make sure I'm still willing to hang out with her, that she still has a best friend in town.

Nevertheless, it's been nice talking to her on a semi-regular basis again.

"Hey!" she sounds excited to hear from me. "What's going on?"

We exchange a few pleasantries, and then I fill her in on the latest Dr. Paige fiasco. I'm expecting her to get a big kick out of it. She usually loves my wacky Dr. Paige stories. But she doesn't react this way. Instead, she's thoughtful.

"That's a really deep observation," she muses. "And I think there's a lot of truth to it."

"Oh, please."

"Think about it, Ry. It's kind of like Noah's song."

"That stupid piece of crap? Whatever. You can't honestly still believe that thing's about me."

"You said so yourself."

"Whatever." I'm eager to change the subject. "Back to Dr. Paige. How on earth can you side with her?"

"Because I think she's right."

"You think, *you actually think*, that I'm making myself

overweight on purpose?" It's the dumbest thing I've ever heard. Who wouldn't want to get thin?"

"Not necessarily on purpose. But just maybe there are some ways that it protects you, like Dr. Paige said."

"That's such crap. How could my weight protect me?"

"There are lots of ways." Chelsea's voice softens. "Think about it, Ry. Think about how much you put off things until you're thin—how much we've both done that. But what if, deep down, we're scared of being skinny? Because then we can't put stuff off anymore. We won't have a good excuse."

I want to argue—my instinct is to argue. But there's a nagging part of me that thinks she might be just a teeny bit right. "When are you coming home, again?" I ask, changing the subject.

"Next week."

"You promise? You're not going to call me at the last minute and say the flight's been changed and you won't be back until two thousand and ten?"

She giggles. "No, no. I'm really coming home this time. For good."

"You swear?"

"I swear."

After we hang up the phone I get back to writing my list.

Chelsea's words keep ringing through my mind. *Because then we can't put stuff off anymore.* We won't have a good excuse. I decide to change up Dr. Paige's assignment a little bit. Instead I make a list of things I put off because I'm fat. Things I insist I would do if I lost weight. This list is so easy to make that it almost feels like cheating. I hope Dr. Paige doesn't hate me for changing her assignment.

## FIVE THINGS I WOULD DO, RIGHT THIS MINUTE, IF I WEREN'T FAT

*1. Stop sugarcoating it and tell Chelsea how hurt I am about the way she's been treating me.*

*2. Make up my mind about college.*
*It would be easier to know where to go if I were skinny. (This might sound weird, but hear me out. NYU is my top choice, but it intimidates me too much. Ditto Vanderbilt. If I were skinny, I wouldn't be intimidated by anything or anyone. My fat pushes me toward, as you would say, the "safe" choice, which is UGA.)*

*3. Tell Josh Lancaster how I feel. Lay all my cards out on the table and admit that I'm developing a huge crush on him.*

*4. Tell <u>everyone</u> how I feel. I rarely stand up for myself, rarely confess what I'm thinking. I walk on eggshells most of the time, bend over backward to please other people because I'm scared of losing them. If I weren't fat, it would be easier to meet people, easier to make more friends if I lost the current ones. If I lost weight, maybe I wouldn't be so scared of people disappearing. Because right now, this is a major fear of mine.*

*5. I know how crazy this sounds, but it's as though all of my relationships are hanging by a thread. I think my weight burdens other people, like it burdens them to be around me, to be friends with me. And I don't want to make the burden any heavier than it already is. I feel like they're already overlooking this giant, overpowering fault (my weight) to be my friend. And I should just shut up, be grateful, and take what I can get.*

# *Freudian Slips*

## DR. PAIGE NORRIS, PhD, MD

PATIENT: *Ryan Burke*

PERSONAL GOALS FOR THE WEEK

1. *Nothing! Enjoy the holidays!*

# Chapter Eleven

CHRISTMAS BREAK IS REALLY BORING. BOTH JOSH and Kimberlee have gone out of town to visit relatives.

They've both called and e-mailed while they've been gone. I'm not surprised about Kimberlee. She and I always talk, on a constant basis. But hearing from Josh was a real shock.

He called me last night, around midnight, and asked if I wanted to go see a new indie movie that's opening the first week in January. It seemed like a random reason to call, but it excited me. Josh and I haven't really hung out much outside of class. This almost feels like a date.

But, of course, it isn't. He's got a girlfriend, remember.

Sigh.

I'm so glad Chelsea will be back. She'll really be here, in the flesh, the day after tomorrow.

I can hardly wait. I just hope her return home doesn't fall through at the last minute. . . .

CHELSEA IS HERE! SHE CALLED ME FROM THE AIRport this morning, told me she'd be over just as soon as she got settled in. "I'll shower, change, and then grab my mom's car keys and come right over."

I felt like this moment would never arrive. But now here it is, four o'clock, and Chelsea's pulling up into my driveway. I stare at her as she steps out of her mother's Altima and walks up the path to my house.

There she is, Chelsea Ramsay, in the flesh. Only she's not the Chelsea Ramsay of five months ago. She's not that Chelsea at all.

"Hey, you!" she squeals.

"Hey," I say, at a loss for words. I'm trying really hard to take it all in, but the image is overwhelming.

She's thin.

Really, *really* thin.

Not only is Chelsea thin, but her hair has been cut and bleached blond—the fucking Gwen Stefani shade of blond that Kim always talks about. And she's wearing a $300 pair of jeans and some T-shirt from a West Coast designer that looks exactly like something I saw Scarlett Johansson wearing on *The Tonight Show* last week.

"I, uh, you look fantastic!" I say, struggling to catch my breath.

"Thanks," she says, smiling. There's that awkward silence, following an unreturned compliment. Although I don't really blame her. She looks so glamorous, stunning. And I look the same as ever.

"You've lost so much weight!" I blurt out.

"About eighty pounds," she tells me, and I'm completely at a loss for words.

We stand there in silence for a moment.

"Give me a hug!" I finally say, enveloping her in my arms.

Chelsea's body feels thin, lithe. "Let's go inside," she says. "I'm dying to see your family."

We wander into the kitchen in search of Mom and Mark. I can't take my eyes off her. I find myself studying every curve of her body . . . which sounds kind of weird and creepy, I guess. But it's not like a gay thing (sorry, Grandpa!). I'm just mesmerized. In awe.

There are no more lumps and bulges; everything is smooth. Her face is still a little round, but other than that, you'd never know she used to be fat at all.

Mark's sitting in the kitchen, eating peanut butter crackers and drinking a glass of grapefruit juice.

"Hi," Chelsea says, beaming. "What's up?"

"Not too much," he says, looking confused. "I'm Mark, Ryan's brother," he explains. "And you are . . . ?"

She bursts out laughing. "Oh, my God! We've known each other for practically forever, you freak!"

It still doesn't dawn on him. "I'm sorry. My memory's a little wasted," he says, smirking. It's true that he doesn't have the sharpest memory around, but I know that's not why he can't place her.

"Uh, this is Chelsea Ramsay," I say. "You know, my best friend."

"No fucking way!" Mark says.

"Yep."

"Mark, watch your language!" my mom calls, coming into the room. When she sees Chelsea, she stops dead in her tracks. She blinks rapidly, doing a double take.

"Chelsea!" Mom shrieks. "I barely recognized you!"

"I didn't recognize her at all," Mark says.

"Come sit down, honey," Mom says, leading her into the living room. "I want to hear all about your time in California . . . and your amazing transformation!"

\* \* \*

F IVE MINUTES LATER, WE'RE ALL SITTING AROUND the fireplace (a useless accessory, considering Atlanta winters are extremely mild) sipping tea (diet Pepsi for Chelsea) and listening to The Story. You know, The Story of How Chelsea Ramsay Got Thin.

"Fat camp," she says, wrinkling her nose. "It was an outpatient thing, although I had my classes and all three of my daily meals there."

Chelsea went to fat camp?

"Ryan never told me that's why you went to California."

Ryan never knew. I feel left out, hurt, misled. Why did she keep such a big secret from me? I tell her everything; I thought she did the same for me.

"It was kind of on the down low," Chelsea explains, sipping her diet Pepsi. "I didn't really want anybody to find out. I wanted to come back and wow everyone."

"You've definitely wowed me," I say, smiling. I'm trying to keep my tone light, friendly. I'm happy for her, don't get me wrong. I just feel hurt that she didn't trust me enough to tell me the truth.

"And I'm going to wow everybody at school next month," she says, her eyes gleaming.

"You certainly will," Mom agrees.

"Big time," Mark chimes in.

The three of them keep right on talking, not noticing how quiet I've been. I keep expecting Chelsea to break away at some point, to suggest she and I go upstairs and catch up. Once in private, I figure, she'll tell me the whole story, fill me in on what's been happening in her life during the past five months. Because, as it stands, I feel like everything I've known was a big fat lie.

Pun totally intended.

But Chelsea only stays for about twenty minutes. When Mom invites her for dinner, she declines. "I've got a Lean Cuisine meal defrosting back home," she says proudly. And I think, damn, is this how she did it? Nothing but Lean Cuisine for five months? Because if that's all it takes to look like this, I'll stockpile the stuff, live on it.

"Besides," Chelsea says mysteriously, "I have a date."

"You do?" I say, unable to keep the surprise out of my voice.

"Yeah, you know Kenneth McClain?" she asks.

"Yes." Of course I do. Everyone knows Kenneth McClain. He's one of the hottest guys at Greenlee, captain of the varsity basketball team, Homecoming escort every year.

"He's taking me to the movies tonight. I think he was pretty excited when he found out about the new me."

"You've been talking to Kenneth McClain?" I ask. *And you told him about the weight loss before you told me?* I add silently. How is this possible that Chelsea has been sharing her secrets with Kenneth McClain, a guy who, for most of her life, was a virtual stranger?

"We ran into each other at the airport," Chelsea explains. "His family was there picking up his uncle for the holidays. Anyway, we got to talking and one thing led to another, and we're going to see that new Jessica Biel movie."

*The romantic comedy*, I think. I remember the trailers. It's the one with the fairytale meeting, the one with all the flirting and the kissing.

Wow. She's going to have a great time.

"Call me later," I say wistfully as Chelsea hugs everyone good-bye and heads out the door.

"Absolutely," she says, giving me a wink. "If I get home early enough."

BUT CHELSEA DOESN'T CALL. I TEXT HER AT AROUND midnight, telling her that I'm not tired, to call whenever she gets in. I know she's just gotten back in town, but she's still on California time, and it's three hours earlier there. That means she'll probably be up late into the night, waiting for sleep to hit her.

Around three a.m., I finally give up, shut off my lamp and TV, and go to bed.

I DO NOT HEAR FROM CHELSEA FOR TWO DAYS. AND EVEN then, it's a hurried call to tell me she's driving down to Florida on Christmas Eve and that she'll be back after New Year's. This shouldn't be a big surprise. She goes to Florida every year to spend the holidays with her grandparents. Still, given how little time we've spent together lately—and how distant things seem between us—I can't help but feel slighted. She promises to call me as soon as she gets back so we can dish on her upcoming (second!) date with Kenneth McClain.

Kimberlee's still out of town, so I wind up spending New Year's Eve with my mother and brother. I could have called around, tried to find something to do, but I kind of enjoy spending the night in with my family.

Oh, my God, that's so sad. But the truth is, it's nice just relaxing, ushering in a new year without too much frenzy.

We eat junk food and watch the countdown on TV. As

midnight approaches, Mom breaks out the Champagne bottle and pours glasses for the three of us. We toast as the ball drops in Times Square.

Another year, come and gone, and I'm still fat.

I'm not big on new year's resolutions, so I don't make any. I prefer to think of myself as a work in progress all year round.

My cell phone starts going mad at midnight. First Kimberlee writes *Happy Fucking New Year!* Then Chelsea, *Having a blast!!! See you soon!* But the one that surprises me the most is from Josh.

*Just hanging out with the fam,* he texts. *Call me if you get bored.*

I want to rush to pick up the phone, call him right then. But I don't want to appear too eager. So I hold out, give it an hour and a half, and just past one thirty I dial his number. I'm kind of excited about talking to him—what a fun way to ring in the new year. But I've waited too long; he must have gone to bed, because his cell phone doesn't even ring, just goes straight through to voice mail.

# Freudian Slips

**DR. PAIGE NORRIS, PhD, MD**

PATIENT: *Ryan Burke*

PERSONAL GOALS FOR THE WEEK

1. *Tell him how you feel. And you know which <u>him</u> I mean!*

# Chapter Twelve

ALL ANYONE AT SCHOOL CAN TALK ABOUT IS CHELSEA.

"She looks so fucking good!"

"Who knew a fatty could be so hot?"

"I wonder how she did it?"

Even Kimberlee, who doesn't go to our school and has only met Chelsea a handful of times, keeps asking me about her. "I heard Ken is going to take her to prom," Kimberlee says the day after we (we being Greenlee High—Kim's school still has another week off) come back from winter break. She picks me up after school so we can hit the mall and catch the post-holiday sales. I invited Chelsea to come along, but she brushed me off.

"Prom is, like, months away!" I say as Kim pulls the car into the long line to get out of the parking lot.

"I know! But he wants to get his bid in early, make sure no one else asks her first."

I wonder if I'll have a date for prom?

"Hey, do you think Josh would want to come shopping with us?" Kim asks, pointing out the window. Josh is standing about five feet away from us, but he looks distracted. He's talking on his cell phone and staring at the ground.

"He looks busy."

"Should I ask him?"

"Nah, let's just go." Kim drives off. The truth is, I don't want to try on clothes while Josh is there. It's one thing to shop with Kimberlee (and that's kind of embarrassing, to tell you the truth). But to charge into Torrid or Lane Bryant in front of Josh would be beyond mortifying.

We don't even end up going to the mall, though. Kimberlee got a new flat-panel TV for Christmas and she wants to shop for DVDs. We wind up at BestBuy, then Circuit City. Afterward, we pop over to Target and browse the sales aisle. By the time we finish, it's late so we grab a bite to eat at Fazoli's and she drops me off back home.

When I get inside, Mom gives me a message. "Chelsea just called."

"Oh, great," I say, reaching for the phone.

"Oh, she said not to bother calling her back. She's going to a basketball game tonight. She'll try you later."

I try her, anyway. Her mom answers, so I leave a message. It's nearly midnight when Chelsea calls me back.

"You should have come to the game!" she says. "It was awesome!"

"You should have invited me."

There's an awkward silence.

"I would have, but you weren't home earlier."

"I have a cell phone," I point out.

"Oh, yeah. I guess I didn't think about it."

Didn't think about it? I've had the same number for two years. She's probably dialed it a million times.

"So did you just get home?" I ask. "I thought the game ended hours ago."

"Oh, it did," she says. "Delia and I went to the mall afterward, and then we grabbed something to eat."

Now I feel really stung. She's hanging out with Delia McConnelly? And they didn't invite me? I don't say anything.

"I know how much you hate shopping with Delia," she rushes on. This is true. Delia always spends forever trying on clothes—in stores that don't carry anything above a size twelve—while I stand around bored.

"But I love shopping with *you*," I say.

"I know . . . ," Chelsea pauses. "But we were going to

Wet Seal, Gadzooks, Express," she tells me. "You wouldn't have liked it."

What she means is, *I wouldn't have fit.*

"Wow," I say. "You're buying stuff at Wet Seal now. Their clothes are so tiny. That's amazing." I try to muster up enthusiasm, but it's hard. I feel left out, like an afterthought.

"Yeah, they have some great stuff." She tells me about her new purchases: tank tops, camis, miniskirts. Everything that would look great on her now.

"So tell me about what's been going on with you," Chelsea says. "I want to hear everything. Photography class, school, Kim—I want to know it all!"

Before I can begin, Chad Michael Murray starts barking in the background. "Uh-oh, I think Duke wants to go out. Let me call you back in ten minutes."

"It's okay. I'm exhausted," I tell her. "We can talk tomorrow."

It's true, I am exhausted. But as soon as we hang up the phone, my mind starts racing. Chelsea's like a totally different person now, with her Wet Seal wardrobe and snazzy new hair. I feel like such an outcast, like I've been left behind.

I toss and turn in bed, lying awake for hours.

\* \* \*

"**I**'M SO GLAD YOU WANTED TO SEE THIS MOVIE," JOSH says as we head into the theater a couple of nights later.

It's Friday—date night. And we're hanging out. But I don't read too much into that. Josh and I are friends. As much as I wish things were more, I know enough not to get my hopes up.

Josh hands me a ticket.

He's paying, which is sweet. We stand in line at concessions. I get a box of popcorn and he buys nachos. I can't believe I'm comfortable enough to eat in front of him but, strangely, I am.

I scan the theater. I halfway expect to see Chelsea here. I talked to her briefly in school today and she mentioned that she was going out with Kenneth this weekend. Again.

"I'm sorry I've been so busy," she said, catching me after homeroom. We don't have any classes together and we're on separate lunch periods, so it's been hard to connect. "But you know how it is. I have tons of makeup work to do, tons to catch up on. That school I went to in Cali"—she lowered her voiced, giggled—"*that fat camp* . . . well, the academics were great, but I'm still not caught up to where I need to be for midterms."

"I could come over this weekend," I offered, "help you study."

"That's okay," she hedged. "I think Kenneth's going to drop by."

"Hey," Josh says, bringing me back to the present, "can you grab some napkins?"

"Sure." I pick up a handful. I'm looking around the lobby when I catch sight of someone waving wildly in my direction.

"Oh, my God, look!" I say, pointing. "There's Megan."

His girlfriend.

"Oh, hey! Come on," Josh says, moving toward her. "Let's go say hi."

I follow behind.

"Meg!" he calls out.

"Hey, baby." She rushes over and gives him a big hug.

"You know Ryan Burke, right?"

"Of course, silly! She and I have homeroom together."

"Oh, yeah!" He smacks himself on the forehead. "Burke, Buford. What was I thinking?"

I'm stunned. All those mornings he's waited outside homeroom for her and he never once noticed me coming out the same door? All this time, I thought he was playing down how well we knew each other so Megan wouldn't get jealous. But in fact, he didn't even care.

"What are you guys seeing?" Megan asks.

*"Nothing."*

She scrunches up her nose. "Yeah, so you just came to the movies to stand around in the lobby and people watch?"

"No, the movie is called *Nothing*," I explain. "It's a Norwegian film. It's in black-and-white, and the cinematography's supposed to be amazing."

"Subtitles." She rolls her eyes. "Those things give me a headache."

"What are you seeing?" Josh asks. I notice his hand is on her lower back, stroking it lovingly.

"The new Reese film," she says. "At least, we will be if Hannah and Lauren ever get back."

"Where'd they go?" I ask, for lack of a better thing to say.

"Bathroom. Gotta touch up their makeup."

"You don't need any," Josh says. "You're beautiful enough without it." He kisses her on the lips, a quick peck, and I shift uncomfortably from foot to foot.

Megan rolls her eyes in my direction. "He's just trying to soften me up so he can get some later," she says conspiratorially.

"So I can come over tonight?" he asks.

"Maybe." She pats him on the head. "If you're a good boy."

I can't even look at them. I hate being in the presence of couples, but this is especially bad. "What time is your movie out?" she asks.

"Probably around ten thirty."

"Well, I'm with the girls until midnight, so you'll have to find something to do until then." She smiles at me. "You can keep him company until then, can't you, Rena?"

"Ryan," Josh corrects.

I just stand there.

"Oh, my God! So Ryan Burke is a girl! I always heard that name on the roll call and I thought it was one of those guys in the back of the room." She giggles.

"Ryan's in my photography course," he says.

"Awesome." She grins. Megan's smile is so wide and so white that it almost blinds me. She's one of those people who show both their upper and lower teeth when they smile. It looks beauty-pageant-fake, the kind of thing she's practiced in front of the mirror. "Josh loves that class."

"I know."

"So can you keep me company for a few hours after the movie? We could grab a bite to eat or something? Go over the contact sheets for tomorrow's class?"

Fifteen minutes ago I would have jumped on this in an instant, but now I can't think of anything less appealing. Sloppy seconds. No thank you.

"I can't. I have to get home early."

"Ah, come on."

"Sorry. Can't do it." I don't give him a reason. I don't even care if it looks rude.

"I'm so glad we got to meet, officially," Megan says, flashing me the unnatural smile again. "I've heard so much about Josh's friend Ryan. And all along I thought you were a boy."

Why does she have to keep saying that? Can't she see I'm not amused? "Well, I'm definitely not a guy."

"I'm really glad Josh has you to hang out with," she continues, ruffling his hair. "Our schedules have been so different this semester, we hardly get to see each other."

"It sucks," he chimes in.

"But I'm glad I've got you around to keep your eye on him." She winks at me. "I always worry what he gets up to when I'm not around. But now that I've met you, it's cool."

"It is?" My voice is almost a whisper. I can't talk or I might start crying.

"Yeah." Megan pats me on the shoulder.

It's okay, yes. Because she is her and I am me. Because I am not a threat. Because I am the fat girl.

"I know he's in good hands," Megan adds, driving the nail in even harder. I feel like I've been punched in the gut.

She knows he would never leave her for me. For a girl like Kimberlee, yes. Or even Chelsea. But guys do not trade in cheerleaders for fat chicks. Maybe in some alternate universe, some Renaissance era, where women are supposed to be Rubenesque and plump. But not here, not in this lifetime.

"We'd better get going," Josh says. "The movie's about to start."

"Can I get a kiss before you go, baby?" she purrs.

He brushes his lips against hers for a quick second. Megan pouts. "A *real* kiss."

I turn away while he frenches her. I can't bear to watch.

JOSH TAKES ME HOME AFTER THE MOVIE. HE BEGS ME to hang out with him, but I refuse. I kind of feel like I might throw up. I want to go home and crawl into bed and fall asleep for the next month.

"It's Friday night," he says as he pulls up into my driveway. "You can't go to sleep at ten o'clock."

"Early day tomorrow," I point out.

"Hey, me too, but you don't see me going to bed this early."

"But that's only because you *have* to stay awake," I practically spit out the words. "To see your girlfriend." *To get your dick sucked*, I add silently.

He doesn't catch the tone in my voice. "So you really won't hang out with me?"

"I have better things to do," I say, pushing open the car door.

"I thought you were just going to go inside and go to sleep?" he teases.

"Yeah," I say icily. "Like I said, I've got better things to do."

I AM TIRED OF BEING THE GIRL LEAST LIKELY TO.

I go into the kitchen and open the freezer. There's a bottle of Aftershock that Mom has hidden behind the ice trays. I don't know why it's in there. I never see her drink from it. I pull the bottle out. It's blood red, with little flecks of ice floating around in it. Chelsea and I snuck a few shots last year and I swear the alcohol level hasn't changed since then.

I grab a coffee mug and pour myself a substantial glass. Then I tuck the bottle under my arm. Screw it. Half the kids in my class are out right now, getting drunk and high and worse. What does this matter?

I take the coffee cup up to my room. The Aftershock smells like cinnamon and goes down like fire. I drink it in two gulps and then nearly fall over from the . . . shock. Ha. I guess it's aptly named after all.

It moves through my veins quickly, hitting me like an IV of liquor. I'm drunk before I even sit down. This is how I need to feel. Relaxed, happy, carefree. I flop back on my bed, throwing my cell phone on the pillow beside me.

I am tired of blaming my fat for everything.

There are five fat girls at Greenlee High—oops, four. I still can't get used to saying that. I can't get used to Chelsea's new physique.

My point is this: The three other fat girls besides me do not live the same life I live. They date. They have sex. They follow their hearts. They get rejected. Why am I doing this to myself? Why can't I just come out and say what I mean? Why can't I tell Josh how I feel?

So what if he rejects me—which he probably will. What will it really matter in the grand scheme of life? Maybe I need to feel something. Maybe I need to get hurt on purpose, hit rock bottom, so I can change.

I pick up the phone and call him.

He answers right away. "Did you change your mind?"

"Come over," I say.

"You want me to pick you up?"

"No." I take a deep breath. I'm finding it hard to speak without stammering. "I. Want. You. To. Come. Over. Here." I pause, gulping down air. I don't think I'm drunk enough. My nerves are still running high. "To my house."

"To your house?"

"Yes. I want you to hang out with me. At my house."

"Ryan, you're acting really strange."

"Just get your little butt over here," I laugh. I almost said, *your cute little butt*. I'm glad I didn't. I have to save something for when he gets here.

"I'm down the street, picking up some drinks," he says. "It'll take a minute."

"Drinks," I mumble. "Drinks are good. I love drinks."

"I can tell." Josh chuckles. "How'd you get drunk this fast? I only left you ten minutes ago."

"Aftershock."

"Whew. That's strong stuff."

"No shit. Are you coming over?"

"I'll come over and stay with you until you sober up, yes."

"But you're bringing more drinks, aren't you?" I exclaim.

"I'm not out getting alcohol, if that's what you mean. I'm eighteen, remember?"

"No fake ID?"

"No."

"Well, bring me a Mountain Dew, then. Or maybe a Coke. What's better with Aftershock?"

"Nothing. You drink it straight."

I climb up off the bed and then teeter over, falling back down. I'm getting drunker by the minute, which is crazy since I haven't had any more Aftershock. I guess it keeps going. Hence the name.

"Ryan? Ryan! Are you there?"

I feel across the floor, reaching for my cell. "Dropped the phone."

"Oh, brother. Okay, hang on. I'll be there in five minutes."

I want to go downstairs and meet him, but my knees feel like rubber. I'm going to kiss him. I've already made up my mind. I'm not going to ask if he likes me; I'm not going to tell him how I feel. I'm too drunk to articulate it. Besides, actions speak louder than words. If I'm going to do this, I might as well go balls in. Sure, the rejection is going to be awful when—*if*—it happens. But at least I'll feel alive.

My cell phone rings a second later.

"I'm at your door."

"Let yourself in," I say. I'm pretty sure it's unlocked.

I hear him clomping up the stairs a second later. "Ryan?" he calls.

"Up here."

Josh appears in my doorway. "You shouldn't leave your house unlocked like that. It's not safe. Especially with your mom and Mark not being home. Where are they, anyway?"

"Mark's thinking about taking some college courses." I hiccup. "They went to an orientation out of town. They'll be back tomorrow." I nearly knock over my drink, then catch it just in time. "Oops."

He sits down on the edge of my bed. "I don't think I've ever been in your room before," he says, looking around.

I sit up, inch closer to him. "You have now."

"I have indeed." He eyes me curiously. "Is everything all right?"

I take another sip of Aftershock. This time directly from the bottle.

"Whoa, whoa, whoa," Josh says, moving closer. He takes the bottle from my hands. "This is really strong stuff, Ryan. You're going to make yourself sick."

I shrug. "Come here for second."

Josh stares at me but doesn't budge.

"No, come over here. I want to tell you something. But I have to tell you when you're closer, because I don't want to say it very loudly."

"Ooooooo-kay," he says, shrugging his shoulders. He scoots across the bed until he's just a few inches away. Perfect.

"You're a really cool guy," I say.

"Thanks. You're cool too."

"But, see, I'm not a guy."

He laughs. "I know that."

"Do you? 'Cause your girlfriend seems to think I'm a freakin' dude."

"Meg's like that, don't take it personally. She's really bad with names and faces unless she knows someone. But now that she's met you, she'll remember you for sure."

"Josh?"

"Uh-huh?"

I've got to do it. It's now or never. Sink or swim. Fail or . . . fail. "Look at me for a sec."

"Okay." He does. His eyes are on mine.

"I want to kiss you." Oh, God, I've said it. I've gone and said it. I feel sick. Here was my big chance to seize the bull by the horns and I've blown it. If I'd gone in for a surprise attack, it might have worked. He might have just gone with it, gotten caught up in the moment. But now I've given him time to think.

"Okay."

"Okay what?" I ask.

"You can kiss me."

I stare at him. "I . . . what?"

"We can kiss."

I don't make a move, so he leans in and does it for me. I'm expecting a peck, so I keep my mouth closed, but then I feel his tongue. I don't know what to do. I'm so confused, disoriented, that I can barely kiss him back. The kiss is good. Intense. Strange. But mostly good. It lasts for a minute or so, and then he pulls away. He looks so calm, as though this is the most normal thing in the world, as though friends do this every day without thinking.

I don't know what this was. A courtesy kiss? A favor? One and done, like Chelsea says? He hasn't moved away, so this time I lean forward and kiss him and, again, he goes with it, kissing me back, hard and then soft, slow and then fast. We're really getting into it and I feel his arms around me, touching my back. I don't want this to stop, I want this to go further. It feels so good, so right.

But Josh stops.

"You want to watch some TV?" he asks, grabbing for the remote.

"No," I say, putting my hand over his. "I want to do this." I kiss him again, but he's less responsive this time. He closes his mouth halfway through and pulls back.

"I don't think we'd better do that anymore."

"What?" I'm baffled. "Why?" I want to ask what I've done wrong, if I'm a horrible kisser or something, but I stop myself.

"I think this is going to keep going, and we don't need to let that happen."

"I'm not that drunk," I tell him.

"Yes, you are."

"If that's what you're worried about . . . that I'll regret it . . . I won't."

"But *I* might."

"You aren't even drinking!"

"I know." He sighs. A big, exasperated sigh.

"When I kissed you, I . . . it's . . . oh, God, I don't know how to explain this."

"Is this because of Meg?" I ask. My lower lip is trembling.

"Partly yes. Partly no." He reaches over and picks up the Aftershock bottle. I wonder if he has to get drunk to do this, to cheat on his girlfriend. I wonder if he'll break up with her. I wonder if he'll tell her what happened. "I'd better go."

"To Megan's," I say scornfully.

"I'm not sure. I might just go home. We have an early class tomorrow." He's being so cold, so distant. "Are you going to be okay?"

"Yes. I'm always okay." I realize, suddenly, that this is the truth. Whatever gets thrown at me, I somehow manage to come out all right in the end.

"I mean you're not going to drink anymore, are you?"

"No," I huff.

"Just the same, I think I'll take this with me." He carries the Aftershock bottle with him on his way out the door. "I'll see you tomorrow morning, Ryan."

And then he leaves.

I can hear Noah's stupid song playing in my mind. *She is not herself these days / Pushes you to go, then stay / She slips from sight, she fades away / Leaves you broken in her wake.*

It describes how I feel about what just happened perfectly.

"He shouldn't have written that about me," I grouse, flopping back on the bed. "It's Josh." I'm not pushing anyone away. I am not sending out mixed signals. I'm here. I'm doing it. I'm putting myself out there. Isn't that what they all said for me to do? Dr. Paige. Kimberlee. Grandpa. My guidance counselor, Ms. Stack. Noah (via his song).

*Wow*, I think. *I was better off before. It's amazing how so many people can be wrong.*

DO NOT GO TO PHOTOGRAPHY CLASS THE NEXT DAY. I can't. Completely irresponsible, I know.

But facing Josh just isn't an option right now.

So I stay in bed all morning. Kimberlee calls a couple of times, but I hit the button to send the phone to voice mail. I've never felt so weird, so depressed, after a kiss. Especially such a *great* kiss.

Around noon, Mom comes to check on me. "The orientation at the college went really well last night," she says. "I think Mark's going to start some business classes in the spring." She looks really proud.

"That's great news," I tell her.

"And maybe he'll take that internship with Grandpa, after all. I think he's scared to try it, but if we give him a little push, he'll be okay."

I can't believe she's going to do this. Push Mark. I never thought I'd hear her say those words.

Mom eyes me carefully. "Are you feeling okay?"

I don't mean to tell her. I really don't. We never talk about this stuff. But somehow I open my mouth and it all comes flooding out.

"Josh Lancaster," she muses, smiling. "I remember when you two were little. Grandpa and I used to always say, 'One day those two will grow up and get married.'"

"Not gonna happen," I say, frowning.

We talk about it for a minute longer and she says, "I think you should go over there. Talk to him. Tell him how you feel."

"I can't do that," I say immediately.

"Why not?"

"I just can't."

"That's your problem, Ryan." She's half teasing, half serious. "You're always on autopilot. You make decisions without thinking them through. You just do whatever the automatic response is."

I stare at her. I'm stunned to hear her say this. "But I'm afraid I'll break down if I try to talk to him."

"No you won't. You'll be fine."

"I could call him," I say, reaching for the phone.

"In person is always better. Always." She pauses. "If Mark can go to college, then you can do this."

She's right. I laugh. "Okay, you've talked me into it. What have I got to lose?" I can think of a million things, but I push them out of my head. "I'm going to go over there, and I'm going to be cool, calm, collected!" I vow.

"That's my girl," Mom says, patting me on the back.

A SHOWER AND A COAT OF MAKEUP LATER, I'M knocking on Josh's front door. It takes forever for him to answer, and I'm starting to worry that he's not home. Maybe he went out with some people after photography class?

Right as I'm about to walk off, the door swings open.

"You!" he exclaims.

I don't know how to take that. I can't tell if he's excited to see me, or merely shocked.

"Can I come in?"

"Of course." He holds the door open and then leads me into the den.

I sit down on the couch. I'd like to stand—I look thinner when I'm standing. But I'm afraid my knees might give out. "About the kiss last night," I begin. "I'm sorry that I did that."

"No, it's okay." He shrugs. "We kissed. It happens."

*It happens?* I can't believe he's being so nonchalant. He

makes it sound like the whole thing was an accident, like our lips just sort of bumped into each other.

"Are you going to, um, tell Megan?" I ask.

"Maybe," he says. "I probably should. We sort of have an agreement about this stuff."

"An agreement?"

He nods. "It's complicated."

"Oh."

"Here." Josh gets up and walks across the room. "I took some notes today in class. That way, you won't get too far behind on what Benji wants." He hands them to me.

"Thanks," I say.

"No problem," Josh says. "Anyway, I have to get going. I'm meeting some friends for lunch, and I'm running late." And then he lets me out the door.

STUMBLE INTO THE HOUSE A FEW MINUTES LATER AND find Mom waiting for me by the front door.

"How did it go with Josh?"

"Not great," I say flatly. "I don't think last night meant very much to him." *I don't think it meant anything, actually.* He was so weird, distant. Unaffected.

She hugs me tightly. "I'm so sorry. You'll have to tell me

all about it in a minute. We'll drown our sorrows in some ice cream and a bad movie."

"Okay."

"But first, you might want to take a look at this," she says, handing me a brown envelope. "You got a registered letter in the mail. It arrived just a minute ago, while you were at the Lancasters'."

When I see the return address, I'm too shocked to speak. It's from Noah!

I rip it open, and a piece of paper and two concert tickets fall out. I sit down on the couch and start to read.

> *Ryan,*
>
> *I owe you an apology. I can't believe I'm putting all of this in writing (my lawyer would kick my ass), but I feel we're better than that. You're better than that.*
>
> *When I talked to you that night, all those months ago, I was a little drunk. Okay, more than a little drunk. I know I'm pulling out the ol' The Vodka Made Me Do It excuse, but it's the truth.*
>
> *When I told you I wrote that song about you,*

*I wasn't lying. Kind of. I'll go ahead and tell you now. Here are the major lines I wrote about you: Give in, 'cause you know you want her / But can you forget their laughter?*

*This is a tough one. When we dated, Ryan, I really liked you. Please don't ever doubt that. You're kind, a great listener, a loyal friend. You're funny, opinionated, smart. But there were things that made me uncomfortable. And I know I'm going to come off like an asshole here, but there was a part of me that was embarrassed to call you my girlfriend. I know that's a terrible thing to say . . . and I don't feel that wayanymore. I'm not perfect, and it was hard for me to hear what people said about your weight. (Even harder to watch how it hurt you.) In some ways, I just wanted to be popular, and dating you didn't fit with that goal.*

*My God, I feel like such a jerk.*

*But I'm only human. It was a stupid, shallow way to act. But I was seventeen at the time. And if I had it all to do over again, I wouldn't care so much about what other people think.*

*Now, about the song. "Girl on Ice" was inspired by a lot of people I've run across in my life. Some of them were important to me. Some of them were not.*

*You were one of the important ones. You really were.*

*I hope that we can still be friends after all this. I'll be coming to Atlanta on tour in the spring and I've enclosed tickets to the show. I hope you'll be there. It would be awesome to see you. And I'd love for you to meet my girlfriend, Julia. I think you'd like her. She reminds me a lot of you.*

*xoxo,*
*Noah*

*PS And I'm sorry that I couldn't call and tell you this. But you know me. I've never been good with the phone. Or in person. In fact, I'm at my best when I'm putting words down on a page. I guess you might have thought I'd have gotten over those fears by now—*

*the public speaking. But I haven't. Ha ha! I guess some things never change.*

No, I think, reading over the last sentence again and smiling. *Some things never do.*

# *Freudian Slips*

## DR. PAIGE NORRIS, PhD, MD

PATIENT: *Ryan Burke*

PERSONAL GOALS FOR THE WEEK

1. *Confront Chelsea.*

# Chapter Thirteen

I AM GETTING OFF ZOLOFT. IT WAS DR. PAIGE'S IDEA. She's been angling for this for a while. She doesn't think I need to be on medication every day.

"We'll try a slow taper," she told me. "If you feel you can't handle it, we can talk about getting you back on it."

So far, I'm handling it pretty well. I'm splitting the pills in half, taking one 25 mg every other day. I was a little dizzy at first, but my depression hasn't returned. I hope that Dr. Paige is right. I hope this is the best thing to do.

"I HAVEN'T BEEN AVOIDING YOU," CHELSEA SAYS, COMING into my bedroom the following Saturday. It's around five o'clock and I'm hanging out with Kimberlee. She's right in the middle of flat-ironing my hair when Chelsea pops in unannounced.

"Because I really haven't," Chelsea continues. "I've just been swamped."

I don't say anything. She's been home for a month now, and she's barely talked to me. This is only the second time she's been to my house. I can count our phone conversations on one hand.

"Why are you here?" I ask. "Did you and Kenneth break up?"

"No . . . why?"

"Because I figured I wouldn't hear from you until that happened."

There's an uncomfortable silence. Kim stands up. "I think I'm going to get a drink," she says, heading downstairs to give us some privacy.

"Ryan," Chelsea starts.

"I don't feel like talking to you."

She looks at me sadly.

"I'm . . . it's been weird lately. I've been weird. I totally admit that. And I understand if you're pissed off at me."

"I'm not pissed off," I tell her. "Just upset."

Chelsea walks over and sits down on the edge of my bed. "Let me explain." She starts talking, telling me about how rough things have been over the past few months. How she wanted to patch things up with her father, how she took a big risk going out there.

"My mom tried to talk me out of it," she says. "She told me it was a terrible idea, that I was wasting my time. And when I got out there, at first things were kind of awful. But my dad started to come around, started to relax a little, stopped being quite so judgmental. By the end of the summer, things were going pretty well. And so when the opportunity came up for me to go to fat camp, it seemed like a pretty good idea."

"Why didn't you just tell me?" I ask.

"I was afraid you wouldn't understand."

"Me?" I ask incredulously. "Not understand? I thought we were BFFFs."

"See, that's just it," she says. "I was taking out the 'fat' part. I was changing things. I didn't know how you'd react."

"You should have told me anyway."

"You're right. I should have." She thinks it over. "I thought you'd think I was a sellout."

"Of course not!" I smile. "I'm just hurt that you kept me in the dark."

"You know, it wasn't my original plan. I was going to just go for the summer, come back in the fall, like I said. But then

I saw the commercials for Camp New You when I got out there, and when I started hinting around to my dad, he agreed to pay for it. And then the whole thing just snowballed."

"It's okay," I tell her. "It was just hard to take. When you came back, it seemed like you didn't have any time for me. Like you'd moved on to bigger and better things."

Chelsea looks hurt. "Oh, God, I'm sorry. I can see how it would come off that way. But you know how it is with Kenneth. He started paying attention to me, and it was so new and exciting that I got completely wrapped up and dropped everything."

I nod.

"And I've loved him since, like, the fifth grade."

"You have?" I ask, surprised. She's never told me this.

Chelsea shrugs sheepishly. "I've loved a whole lotta guys since fifth grade. I just haven't ever gotten any of them. Until now."

The words hang in the air for a minute, and they're a little sad. My love life has never been fantastic, but at least I've had dates, made out with guys. Chelsea's been practically Amish.

"So, tell me, what's been up with you?" she asks.

"Ha." I laugh. "Have you got an hour?"

"I have, like, twenty-four." She smiles. "I told Kenneth I'm taking some time away from him. You know, don't want to get burned out too quickly." She pauses. "But I know you've got Kimberlee over, so do you want to hang out another time?"

"Hang on." I run downstairs and find Kimberlee. "Do you mind if Chelsea hangs out with us tonight?" I ask.

"Are you kidding?" she says, grinning. "After all the stories I've heard—the body shots in Hollywood, the crazy makeover—I've been dying to get to know this chick!"

I laugh. Later that night, as we settle down to watch a movie, I notice the bottle of Zoloft on my nightstand. I haven't taken one in a week. I was so afraid to stop taking them, but I feel fine. No, better than fine. I feel great. Maybe even fantastic . . .

CHELSEA AND KIM WIND UP SPENDING THE NIGHT. We stay up for hours talking. Things are still a little strained at points. . . . It's not how it used to be with Chelsea, at least not yet. But it's good that we're on the right track.

I didn't get much sleep the night before, so I'm taking a nap when I hear a knock outside my bedroom.

"Ryan?"

"Huh," I mumble.

"Can I come in?" I recognize the voice, but in my sleepy state, I can't place it.

I sit up, flip on the bedside lamp. "Hello?"

"It's Josh."

Whoa. What is he doing here? Ever since our talk last week, things have been awkward. I saw him yesterday morning in photography class, but we barely said two words to each other.

"Hang on!" I scramble out of bed, throw off my pajamas, and climb into a pair of jeans and a sweater. "Okay, you can come in."

He opens the door, sticks his head in tentatively. "I'm sorry if this is a bad time. Mark let me in."

"It's okay," I say, suppressing a yawn. I sit down on my bed, trying to act casual. "What's up?"

"I wanted to talk to you about something."

"Okay."

"About that, uh, line we crossed the other day."

I shake my head. "The line *I* crossed," I correct him. As much as I wish this whole thing was mutual, I realized pretty quickly: Josh was just playing along, going with the flow, letting me have my moment. "I crossed a bunch of lines, actually. I screwed up our friendship. I made you cheat on Megan. . . ."

He sits down beside me on the bed. "First of all, you didn't *make* me do anything. I kissed you back, remember? No one forced me to do that."

I can't look at him. I stare down at my feet, the floor.

"And that's what I wanted to tell you." He sighs. "I can tell you've been feeling bad about that, but I actually wasn't cheating. Meg and I . . . we can kiss other people. It's her rule, not mine. She made it a few months ago. She always claimed that she doesn't consider kissing cheating. But, truthfully? I think she was bored with me. She wanted some more adventure, more variety in her life."

I can't imagine anyone getting bored with Josh, but I don't say anything.

"I've always suspected she's done stuff behind my back. And when she instituted the kissing rule, it just fueled that."

"Oh." I'm not really sure how to respond to this. It seems like a weird way to have a relationship. Either break up or date exclusively. I've never been a fan of the middle-ground stuff.

"Not that any of this matters." He stops. "I broke up with her last night."

"What?!" So much for cool, calm, and collected.

"Look . . . ," his voice trails off. "I've known something wasn't right with me and Meg for a while now. I guess it just took this to help me see that."

I can't speak now. I can only stare at him.

"And with what happened last weekend, you shouldn't feel so down on yourself." He seems hesitant. "I just wasn't sure whether it was the right thing to do . . . but I wanted to. I kind of . . . God, I feel like such a geek saying this, but I kind of like you."

"You do?"

"Yeah." He chews on his lower lip. "But it's weird. Because we're friends."

*And because I'm fat?* I wonder. *Is it weird because I'm fat?* I push the thought out of my head. He's sitting here, smiling at me, saying these things, and all I can think about is my fat? As soon as something good happens in my life, I start trying to break it down, find all the reasons why it's destined to fall apart.

"I like you, okay." Josh laughs softly. "It's weird for me to say this, but I do." He seems so genuine, so sweet. I stare at him.

Is it possible that he really likes me, fat and all? Wants to be with me, me over Megan Buford? It's like Kerry Vance and Ava Peeler, all over again.

Then again, maybe I'm selling myself short. Maybe I've been on an even playing field all along. Maybe I just never knew it before now.

But I don't have time to think about all this, because the next thing I know, Josh is kissing me again. It's soft, gentle, every bit as amazing as I remember. We hold it for a minute, then break away.

"Wow," I say.

"Wow."

He puts his hand on mine, traces his fingers over my palm.

"So are we going to . . . ?" I ask, my voice trailing off. "I mean, is this . . . are we . . ."

Josh raises an eyebrow. "What are you trying to say?"

"Are we going to become, like, a couple?"

"Let's see what happens," he says, smiling. "I don't like to get too far ahead of myself. But I was thinking, though, that I'd like to go out with you sometime. If you're up for it."

"I am," I say, squeezing his hand and leaning toward him. "Anytime."

# Epilogue

I T'S THE NIGHT OF NOAH'S CONCERT IN ATLANTA. AND here we are, sitting in the fourth row: Me, Josh, Chelsea, Kenneth, and Kimberlee. (When I contacted Noah, he was kind enough to get me three extra tickets.)

We all had lunch today before the show. It was great seeing him again. I introduced him to Kimberlee, reintroduced him to Chelsea and Josh. Noah even brought his new girlfriend, Julia. She's great—sweet and kind and beautiful. All the things he deserves.

"You and Josh seem really tight," Noah whispered in my ear when we were finished eating. "I bet you'll be together for a long time."

"Maybe," I said, giggling. I was giddy at the thought. Things are going great now—have been for two months. But I don't want to get carried away.

I can't really say what the future holds. I guess I'm not

as good at predicting things as I'd thought. If you'd asked me sixth months ago, I never would have believed any of this was possible. I wouldn't have believed that Mark would sign up for college (he starts this fall!). I wouldn't have believed that Kim and I could become so close, that Chelsea would remake herself. . . . I wouldn't have believed Josh.

A song comes on, one of Noah's older tracks, and we all sing along. It's a soft ballad, and everyone in the crowd is holding up cell phones and lighters, illuminating the arena.

"This is great," Josh says, nudging me softly.

"I know," I tell him. "It is." And I mean it. I even mean it, five minutes later, when "Girl on Ice" comes on. Wow, it's so weird. A few months ago, I'd never have imagined us all here together. I'd never have imagined myself singing along to *this* song.

But I do. And it's amazing.

Anyone who tells you they've got it all figured out is lying. We can't predict the future. We have to take it as it comes.

And right now, it's coming fast and furious.

I just got my acceptance letter in the mail from NYU, and I'll be starting school there in the fall. It's amazing how easy it all turned out to be. I worried for so long, worried that I'd make the wrong decision. And, in the end, as I sealed my application for NYU, I knew it was the right thing. I knew it was what I wanted.

I want a lot of things now, and I'm not afraid to go for them.

Like with Josh. Telling him how I felt had once seemed impossible, but I'm so glad I took that chance. We're together now, and so far, things are . . . magical. A cheesy way to describe it, I know, but it's hard to think about him without feeling giddy inside.

It seems like something great is starting here, something that was meant to be. You know, planets lining up, and all that crazy stuff.

"It's funny," Josh said, when I told him about NYU this morning, "we're both moving almost a thousand miles away, but we'll still be neighbors."

I laughed when he said this. "You know, you're right."

"I guess it's true," he said, kissing me softly on the lips. "Fate has a weird way of bringing people together."

"Yes," I said, kissing him back. "It definitely does."

# About the Author

J O EDWARDS IS THE BESTSELLING AUTHOR OF THREE adult novels. She is an award-winning journalist who has been featured in *USA Today*, *Us Weekly*, and the *Boston Globe*, among others.

Jo currently lives in Memphis, Tennessee. She would like you to know that she has never met Elvis (he died before she was born) or Justin Timberlake. Jo loves partying, shopping, and television, although she balances this out by reading things like *The Economist*. She is also an avid traveler and once lived in London for a year. When Jo isn't writing, she can usually be found drinking way too much iced coffee, hanging around bookstores, or watching reality TV.

Visit her website at www.joedwardsbooks.com.

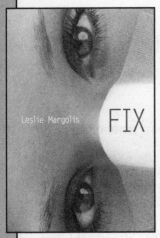
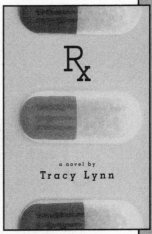
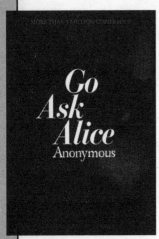

# Girls searching for answers . . . and finding themselves.

# In the beginning ... there was a plan.
# And the plan was good.

**THE HACK:**
Get a slacker into Harvard.

**THE CREW:**
Three nerds and a beauty queen.

**THE PLAN:**
Take down someone who deserves it.
Don't get distracted. Don't get caught.

**THE STAKES:**
A lot higher than they think.

You don't need to be brilliant

You just need a plan.

HACKING HARVARD

a novel by Robin Wasserman

# HACKING HARVARD
## by Robin Wasserman

- - - - - - - - - - - - - - - - - -

From **Simon Pulse**

Published by Simon & Schuster